@SAPHIRAHOLZKEN

# Little Miss SANTA CLAWS

BEKA WESTRUP

First published in the United States of America November 2024 by Beka Westrup

Cataloging-in-Publication Data is on file with the Library of Congress.

ISBN: 979-8-9863087-9-1 (paperback), 979-8-9918870-0-7 (e-book)

Author website: https://www.bekawestrup.com

Editor: Alexa Thomas (The Fiction Fix)

Cover Art: Sarah (@moonrosesxart on Instagram)

Cover Design: Eternal Geekery (@eternalgeekery on Instagram)

Internal Art (cabin art): Saphira (@saphiraholzken on Instagram)

# Playlist

1. Call it Dreaming - Iron & Wine
2. Santa Tell Me - Ariana Grande
3. Good Cry - Noah Cyrus
4. 3 Minutes - JP Saxe
5. Jingle Bell Rock - aespa
6. live more & love more - Cat Burns
7. Snow On The Beach - Taylor Swift
8. Turn On The Lights - Jamie Cullum
9. There's No Way - Ian McConnell & Morgan Johnston
10. Devil in Her Eyes - Bryce Savage
11. Are You Gonna Be My Girl - Jet
12. Lights On Kind of Lover - Maddie Zahm
13. Christmas Don't Be Late - Norah Jones
14. Birch (feat. Taylor Swift) - Big Red Machine

# Content Warnings

- Alcohol Use
- Depictions of Anxiety/Panic Attacks
- Themes of Grief/Loss
- Explicit Sexual Content

*For the shameless krampus-lovers*

# CHAPTER 1

# *Nicole*

I hate that princess movies always end on the wedding day. With one long, romantic kiss, their fates are sealed with a pretty bow that reads *The End*, and we're all supposed to believe they live happily ever after in marital bliss.

There's no such thing.

It's during The *After* when real life happens—the boring and hard and ugly—and those movies did a huge disservice to little girls everywhere by making us all think otherwise.

In real life, there's always an after, and it's rarely ever happy.

My ringtone fills the corners of my mother's gaudy, stale living room as dust sparkles in the rays of sunlight pouring through the windows. This is at least the twelfth time work has called me today. On Christmas Eve, no less. But when you work in upper management at a thriving toy manufacturer, such is to be expected. People probably think our hardest work ends by Christmas day, but that couldn't be further from the truth. It's shocking how many parents wait until the last possible second to purchase something. In fact, we sell just as many units the day after Christmas as we do the weeks before, thanks to a little thing I like to call the "split-family effect." This is the busiest week of the year for me, which is perfectly fine. It's not like I have anything else in my life that needs my undivided attention right now—or any*one,* for that matter.

Whatever. It's fine.

I'm *fine.*

I wonder how many times I need to tell myself that before I start to believe it. Probably a handful more, at the very least. *Rewire those thoughts, Nicole.* I hear my therapist's chipper voice singing in my head. Like a carousel, her words come back around, around, around. I know they're true; I just don't like being told what to do.

Speaking of being bossed around...

My mother turns to glare at me from where she stands beside the fake Christmas tree. The plastic fringe is balding in places, and a quarter of the lights have burnt out. For some reason, she refuses to replace the ancient, off-white thing. She just piles on a couple extra cartons of ornate glass ornaments to fill the empty space. I guess she thinks covering it up will hide the disrepair.

If that isn't the most succinct assessment of my mother I've ever thought up, I don't know what is. It's actually making my stomach hurt.

Although the stomach ache could be thanks to the bran muffins Mom forced down my throat earlier. They're currently slugging through my intestines in a very painful way. We should be eating real bread and sugary casseroles and peppermint sweets, just for a couple of days. I'd cut out my own kidney for even a sliver of apple pie at this point.

Okay, that was a little dramatic, I'll admit.

But seriously, it's Christmas, and I hate her food. I was free from her "cooking" for an entire blissful decade, but then I was forced back home a month ago due to my romantic failures. I think that makes it worse, knowing what I'm living without. My freedom. My kitchen. The life I created.

All of it is just...*gone*.

I return my gaze to my phone and silence the call before I pull up my messages and send a text to the co-worker calling. I'd rather not expend what very little social energy I have left on a phone call. As I tap away on the screen, I hear my mother let loose a frustrated sigh.

"Are you alright, Mom?" I say through tight lips. "Do you need me to grab you another Xanax from the medicine cabinet?"

"Don't antagonize me, Nicky."

I grind my teeth, continuing to type. I've told her a million times how much I hate that nickname, but she still uses it. I haven't been Nicky in a long time. In a cold voice, I reply, "I didn't realize I was being antagonistic. I was just offering to help."

"What would be *helpful* is you getting off your phone and decorating the tree with me. I'm doing this for *you*. I'm not even going to be here tomorrow to enjoy this, but I'm setting it all up anyway. The least you could do is appreciate the effort I'm making."

No, she won't be here.

She's going to be in Wyoming, spending Christmas with my sister and her family, and I'll be here. My first Christmas *entirely* alone. No one thought to extend a Wyoming invitation to me.

On one hand, I understand that my homecoming was abrupt. I haven't spent Christmas around my sister in years, so I understand why I wasn't invited. On the other hand...I didn't want to spend Christmas by myself. That's why I moved home when my husband asked for a divorce.

I don't know what I was thinking. I would have been better off sleeping on my friend's couch back in Cincinnati.

Hope is a vicious thing, especially when it's crushed before it has an opportunity to flourish. I sell childish joy year-round, but inside, right now, I feel completely bankrupt.

With a deep breath, I put my phone down and sit a little straighter—battle position at the ready. "I didn't ask you to do this, Mom. You didn't have to set up the tree. I'm starting to think it might be easier to just pretend Christmas doesn't exist this year."

She rolls her eyes and sets her hands on her hips. "You were the one complaining just last week about it not feeling like Christmas around here."

"Because you moved to Florida. There's no snow."

"I moved to Florida because it's warm and the people are nice. If you wanted snow, you should have vacationed somewhere else."

"This isn't a vacation," I grumble.

"Yes, *clearly*. You're a workaholic, Nicky. You're on your phone constantly. I'm right here, and you barely look at me. It's really no mystery why your marriage didn't work out."

My heart skips in my chest. "Wow," I exhale. "Okay. I'm not going to sit here and let you talk to me like this."

I shove the fuzzy blanket off my legs and stand, heading for the arch leading into the rest of the house. Sure, I refused to explain why I was getting a divorce when I came home. I didn't want to talk about it. But how could she just assume it was my fault? And after she went through the exact same thing—*twice*. I'd definitely made the wrong decision coming here.

This isn't even really *home* to me. I grew up a handful of states away, but it's not like I could go there. The only people I know who still live there are my sister and my father, and they have their own families to take care of now.

Unfortunately, I can't afford to go anywhere else, not until I can pay my divorce lawyer off.

The best I *can* do is hide away in the guest room until my mother leaves and then run to the grocery store before they close. I could use some liquor and candy.

But as I'm leaving the room, she calls after me, "And so you run away from me, just like you ran away from Matt. If you wanted to work things out, you should have stayed and fought for it. People make mistakes, Nicky."

Something dark and foreign surges within me. It's a culmination of everything I've bottled up over the last few years, and her words activate it like yeast in rising dough. It's brimming over. I can't hold it anymore as I spin on my heel.

"There was nothing left worth fighting for. I was *always* the one to sacrifice in our relationship—time and money and more than that. I gave him everything. We moved to Cincinnati for *him*, for *his* career. When he wanted to go back to college, I supported him. Then, when he dropped out and decided to switch careers to something that kept him traveling for months at a time, I supported him. When I found out he was cheating on me and he swore it was a one-time mistake, I forgave him, all because I wanted to *work things out.*

"He didn't make a mistake. Everything he did to hurt me was intentional. My staying with him for that long was the real mistake. He didn't want me. I was just convenient. I was there, so he kept me, like a fucking pet or something. The moment he found a way out of our marriage, he took it. So yeah, I am working a ton, but that's because I passed up so much professionally for that man, and he gave me absolutely nothing. I'm taking what I need now. I did run away, and it was long past time for me to do so."

Once it's out, I feel both better and worse. My throat hurts and my eyes sting.

All I said was true, but I didn't include that I was done too. For months, I was done with our marriage, just going through the motions, and I think Matt knew that. He could see it, feel it. So even though I know logically that the demise of our relationship wasn't on me, I still feel at fault for the final severing.

I stare at my mother and grimace at the pity on her face.

I'd finally gotten some compassion, but it didn't make a difference. Maybe her compassion wasn't really what I wanted.

She sighs and walks over to me, raising her hands to my upper arms and firmly squeezing. A little bit of affection to mask the hurt. It feels like she's spreading spackle over a massive crater. "I didn't mean to make you upset, Nicky. Let's just...finish decorating the tree together, okay? I have to leave for my flight soon."

That was as close to an apology as I would ever get from her.

My face burns. I'd exploded, and her calmness makes me feel crazy. Maybe I'm being irrational. Maybe I let my emotions get the best of me.

I nod weakly. "Fine."

She gives me a brittle smile and leads us back to the tree.

I pick up a blue star ornament from the plastic storage tub and turn to hang it up, wishing I could feel even one iota of Christmas cheer.

# CHAPTER 2

# *Nicole*

I sit cross-legged in the living room on top of my mother's pristine faux fur rug. All month, she has been adamant about keeping food away from it, but she's not here to gripe at me tonight. I have an array of cheap gas station snacks laid out on top of it: chips and chocolate and a full lemon meringue pie. I'm eating it straight out of the tin.

Bran muffins, you can eat my ass.

A feel-good Christmas movie is playing on the tv. Turns out, I'm just not capable of pretending this holiday doesn't exist. Half a bottle of peppermint schnapps in, I caught myself humming *Jingle Bell Rock*, and it was all downhill from there. The tears won't stop flowing.

I'm blaming it on the somewhat surprising emotional depth of the movie and the fact that the love interest looks a little bit like Matt.

*"... don't you see? I love you. All I want for Christmas is you..."*

I'm right back at the altar, my hands in Matt's and our entire future ahead of us. I believed every word of his vows, even though there had been a certain apathy in his eyes I chose to ignore. There were a dozen red flags I buried during our marriage. Little did I know, I was preparing a graveyard for "us."

My sadness bleeds into rage, and I chuck the half-eaten pie across the room. It hits the center of the screen in an explosion of lemony cream. "*YOU LIAR*," I sob. The characters continue kissing each other under the smear of pie, unbothered by my outburst.

I crawl to the remote and quickly turn off the television.

"Stupid," I murmur to myself.

The living room falls deafeningly silent. It's worse than the movie. My head spins as I look around the room, lit only by the Christmas tree. The world outside is dark; one tiny bulb on the right side of the tree is flickering, and my eye twitches as I stare at it. I should have told my mother no. I shouldn't have let her talk me into it. Decorating the tree with her has sent me spiraling, and I'm more worked up now than I was earlier.

The divorce weighs on me.

It's not that I'm losing Matt. It's that I'm losing years of my life to what turned out to be the wrong person. How could I have thought he was right?

I bet my mother's plane touched down already. I bet she's setting out cookies and milk for Santa and helping my sister tuck my niece and nephew into bed. She's going to wake up in the morning surrounded by laughter and excitement and joy. My father is too. Even Matt is with his parents and siblings right now. Everyone has somebody to share Christmas with—everyone except me.

The decorations and food and music and movies are all worthless. They mean nothing.

Before I even realize I've decided to do it, I push myself up off the floor. I retrieve a storage tub from the garage and start tearing every ornament off the tree. My tears are flowing again. I can barely see through them.

When the tub is full, I pick it up and waddle over to the front door, pausing in the kitchen to toss the rest of the bran muffins in. Then, I drag the ornaments around the side of the house, out of view of the street, and dump them out on the grass.

I'm wearing nothing but flimsy sleep shorts and a tank, but I'm not even cold.

I hate that. It's the middle of the night on Christmas Eve. I *should* be freezing my ass off, but no, the air is barely cooler than it is during the day. It almost feels like a summer night back in Cincinnati. I'm reminded of the first summer Matt and I spent there as newlyweds, when the *I love you*s were innumerable and we both meant them. The memories solidify my drunken resolve, and I stumble my way through the back door of the garage.

Grabbing a metal rake, I return to the ornaments and don't hesitate to start smashing them.

I swing the tool with all my strength, bringing it down over and over. I work up a sweat, continuing to smash the beautiful hand-spun glass, delighting in the crunch. Some of my dark brown hair slides free from my bun, but I keep going, even after every ornament has been destroyed. Minutes or hours could have passed when I finally stop, letting the rake fall on top of the wreckage.

I'm sober again.

Sober enough to regret what I just did to my mother's ornament collection. They're barely recognizable. All the little metal tops are dented, and the glass shards are covered in brown pulp from the muffins.

I raise my trembling hands to my face, fingernails digging into my forehead as I cover my eyes. "*Fuck.*"

There's no fixing or replacing them. My mother has spent most of her life collecting those ornaments. She probably loves them more than she loves me—not an exaggeration—and I just...destroyed them.

Holy fuck, I am a total loser.

Maybe Mom's right. Maybe everything is my fault. Maybe I sabotaged my marriage without even realizing it. That's how it always happens, right? Self-destructing tendencies override conscious thought or whatever? Maybe I pushed Matt into distancing himself, into a job that kept us apart, into affairs that made him feel the love I couldn't give him, the love he needed. Maybe I was the problem all along.

I've never needed my therapist more in my entire life, but I've been avoiding our sessions all month and I certainly can't call her with my problems now. Not on Christmas.

Besides, she'd probably just tell me not to be so hard on myself.

But she doesn't see this side of me. No one does.

My knees feel like they're on the verge of giving out, so I crouch, sitting on the back of my heels as I stare hopelessly at the mess I've made. It makes sense now—why my family didn't want me in Wyoming. Why my father didn't want me. Why they all turn away. How could anyone want someone like me when I do stupid shit like this?

I can't fix these ornaments, and I can't fix *me*.

I'm sinking deep under that torrential storm of emotion when I hear a thud above me. My head snaps up—because I think it...came from the roof. The sky is pitch black with a faint speckling of stars, a cloud moving across the moon, making it too dark to see much, especially from this angle.

I stand and back up a couple of steps, but that isn't quite enough to see onto the roof.

Another loud thud echoes, accompanied by strained

hissing whispers, and I nearly leap out of my skin. That's when I realize I'm standing outside in my thin nightclothes with nothing but a rake to defend myself with.

A woman hearing strange noises on the roof when she's home alone over the holidays? It sounds like the beginning of a really strange horror movie.

I snatch the rake and press it to my chest as I sprint back to the front door.

When I'm inside, I turn the deadbolt before I run through the kitchen to do the same thing to the garage door. It makes me feel the tiniest bit better, but for some reason, my fingers tighten on the rake anyway. Something feels different in the house...like I'm not alone.

The back of my neck tingles.

My ragged breathing feels too loud in my ears, and it takes me an agonizing few moments to realize the sound isn't my breathing at all. It's *rustling*.

Something is rustling in the living room.

For the first time since I arrived in Florida, my body feels like a block of ice. I'm frozen to the spot, my thoughts racing as I try to figure out what I should do. It couldn't be a person, could it? I didn't see another vehicle on the street next my mother's. Maybe it's just an animal. Mom warned me about that—the animals that get into houses around here. I might have left the front door open, but I can't remember.

If it is an animal, particularly a dangerous one, then I'll need my phone to call someone—which is sitting on the decorative table near the entrance to the living room.

I force myself to take a step forward, then another.

Walking slowly, I make my way to the edge of the kitchen, nearing the arch into the living room until I can finally peer around it.

What I find knocks the breath out of my lungs.

It's a person. There's a person in my mother's living room. They're wearing an oversized red coat with the most beautiful brown fur lining the collar. A red cap sits on their head, with a long tail and a brown puff hanging at the end made of the same fur. They look like Santa Claus.

My mother's house has been broken into by a goddamn Santa impersonator.

A surprised gasp leaves my lips before I can stop it, and the person turns toward me. That's when I see that it's not a man—it's a woman. A beautiful woman with straight silver hair and piercing blue eyes. And she's clutching the bag of cookies I left on the rug, her mouth full of them.

Her eyes bulge, and she swallows hard before whispering, "Oh, sugar plums."

The woman's voice snaps me out of my daze, and I stagger back, spinning around to make a break for the door. But as I do, I trip over one of the fake plants my mom left at the corner of the archway, and I'm suddenly falling face-first toward the floor, the pointed tips of the rake staring me down. I scramble to catch myself, throwing the rake away, but that only makes me trip again on the handle.

And the last thing I hear before my head collides with the wall is a stampede of tinny bells chasing after me.

# CHAPTER 3

# Nicole

When I come to, I can tell I haven't been out long. I even remember what was happening *before* I whacked my head hard enough to see stars. But the problem with knowing how I lost consciousness is knowing exactly what the source of those tinkling bells is.

The air shifts as I listen to the beautiful intruder kneel beside me.

She's mumbling frantically under her breath. "No, no, no. This can't be happening."

It takes everything in me not to react when her hand brushes against my forehead. I bite the inside of my lip to keep from moaning at the ache in my head. What do I do? Why is she still here? What does she want?

"Ah, *Mother-elfing Frost*," she says, the words breathy and forceful, as if she's swearing. I feel her hands on my face again. Her skin is so cold, but soft too. Velvety. "Please wake up. Please be okay. I'm sorry I scared you like that. You were supposed to be asleep."

Her worry softens the edges of my panic. Even if she is a thief, she's clearly not violent.

A muted thud vibrates down from the roof, and the tiny woman beside me growls up at the ceiling. "Blitzen, you better *simmer down* up there."

My brow furrows despite myself.

Blitzen? Like...the reindeer? What the fuck?

Wait. I hear that thudding too. There really *is* something on top of the roof. The question is: what? Because it sure as hell can't be reindeer. Is there another person here?

I hear a wild squeak beside me as the intruder's hands tilt my face toward her, and I know my pinched expression must have given me away.

"Oh, thank goodness," she squeals. "You're waking up. Are you okay? Please tell me you're okay. Are you in pain? Can you hear me? Do you know where you are? Here." Her hands leave my face. "Can you tell me how many fingers I'm holding up?"

Man, this girl can talk, and really fast. Which isn't a bad thing, exactly. Her voice is kind of nice, actually, all husky and warm.

Reluctantly, I peel my eyes open.

She's leaning over me, her head haloed by the Christmas tree lights. She has plump, rosy cheeks and a bulbous little nose. Her eyes are wide and watery, glittering a dark blue in the shadow cast over her face. She's even more beautiful at a second glance. *Gorgeous.*

Seeing as she breaks into people's houses for a living, I'm sure that helps. Who wouldn't want to go easy on a face like that?

Unfortunately for her, I'm having a really shitty night.

I take a deep breath and lurch upright, bracing my arm against her chest to knock her backward. She topples with another high-pitched squeak, and I scramble through the archway into the living room to retrieve my phone. I scoop it up and tap on the black screen, but it doesn't light up. I tap a few more times, trying to coax it awake. Jingling bells alert me to the fact that the intruder is standing back up, and I press the power button on my phone, only to see an empty power icon appear.

My phone is *dead*.

"Shit, shit, shit," I whisper.

The woman appears in the archway, her cap lopsided and eyes narrowed in displeasure. "That was *very* naughty of you, Cynthia. To think, I brought you a present." She points at me as she stalks forward, and her cherub-like features start to look downright sinister. "I get that this job doesn't allow for a lot of personal interaction, but I think I deserve a little elfin' respect on delivery day."

Alarm bells ring through my head.

Never mind. This woman is totally nuts, and now I've angered her. She could be dangerous.

I hold the phone screen to my chest as I back up into the center of the room. "Look," I start tremulously. "I don't know what you're doing here or who you think I am, but you have the wrong girl. You have the wrong house. Please leave."

Her eyes turn black. "No, I don't think I will. I think you owe me an apology."

"An apology?" I scoff. *No fucking way.* "*You* are the one breaking and entering, which is a *federal offense,* by the way. I'm not apologizing for shit. I already called the cops, so you better hurry up and call your friend on the roof so you can both fuck right off before they get here."

She takes one slow, menacing step toward me. "You didn't call the police."

"Of course I did." My throat swells as I retreat another step. "They're on the phone right now."

The smile that spreads over her face is grotesque, her face

looking like it's literally morphing before my eyes—her teeth elongate and sharpen to points, her skin pales and takes on a silvery sheen, and her eyes sink into her face until they look like hollows void of all light.

I stagger backward until I hit the Christmas tree. My breath catches in my throat as I realize I must have given myself a concussion. I'm seeing things now.

"Do you think Santa Claus can't tell when you're lying?" she sneers. "I can. Now, make it up to me by getting on your knees."

My heart skips a beat. "Excuse me?"

"Get. On. Your. Knees. And then maybe I'll forgive you."

A disbelieving laugh bubbles out of me. She has a real fucked-up sense of humor.

Her hands glide up and part her coat before dropping to her hips. She has a belt of small brass bells and a skin-tight red shirt with buttons lining the center, open halfway down to her sternum. When I lift my gaze back to her face, I see she's still frowning at me.

My God. I think she's actually serious.

"No," I gasp. "I'm not going to do that."

She doesn't react, doesn't move or breathe or blink. She just continues to stare at me with those terrifying eyes, unwavering, and I find myself...dropping to my knees. Because this woman scares me. The sooner I apologize, the sooner she'll leave. I hope.

When my knees hit the floor, she sashays up to me, pausing a foot or so away. Her teeth are back to normal now, and there's a little more pink in her cheeks.

"Kiss my boots," she demands in a soft voice.

My lips part, and my cheeks warm as her eyes burn into mine. I glance down at the black leather boots on her feet. They're freshly polished, with golden buckles glimmering up the length of her calves. She's a small thing, but the boots make her look tall. I don't know where those boots have been tonight, and she wants me to *kiss* them?

I shift my glare up to her face. "Are you insane?"

Her eyes flash black again as a guttural growl wraps around me. A blast of icy wind sweeps through the air between us, lifting her silver hair in an ethereal fan. The skin of her face turns sallow and gray as her black and red nails extend into claws. *What the fuck is going on?* "What do you think? Is this better? How *insane* do I look to you now?"

I lean as far back as I can, and a few of the tree branches dig into the back of my head. "Stop," I whisper. "Please."

"You know how to make this stop."

Gritting my teeth, I slowly force myself to lean forward, bending at the hips. As I close the distance between my lips and her boots, the overwhelming scent of pine and fresh cookies fills my nostrils.

Where the hell has she been? A bakery in the forest?

My pride punches through my throat and scrapes the back of my eyes. It's best just to do it quick. Get it over with.

I squeeze my eyes shut and lower my lips the rest of the way, kissing one and then the other boot. When I sit up, my heart skips, thumping harder. She's smiling at me. Her skin is pink and soft and lovely again, and her eyes are a brilliant, sparkling blue.

As I sit in her sudden warmth, she raises an eyebrow, and I remember my groveling isn't complete.

"I-I'm sorry," I stutter. "I'm sorry for pushing you before."

"And?" she drawls.

"I'm sorry for—uhm, lying to you."

"*And?*"

My brow stitches as I replay the last few minutes in my head. "And for...calling you crazy?"

Her domineering stance melts away, her smile pulling even wider as she braces her hands on her knees and leans over me. "There we go. Good girl. Don't you feel better? I certainly do." She chuckles to herself as she straightens. "If you'll excuse me, I have three more continents to deliver to before dawn. Good night, Cynthia. Enjoy your present."

She spins around, and I'm left reeling as she rifles through the pockets of her coat.

That coat she's wearing is more than oversized—it's just plain too big for her. The bright red coattails drag on the ground, and I can see they've been dragging for a while. They're damp and dirty, and that is *definitely* a pine needle stuck to one side.

I should be angry with her, disgusted by the way she humiliated me. But for some reason, I'm not. I feel more in control. I do feel *better*.

I'm so fucking confused.

Her movements become a little more frantic as she roots around in her pockets for a second time. "Where is that thing?"

"Hold on. My name isn't Cynthia," I murmur, still feeling a bit dazed.

The intruder's body stiffens. After a long moment, she turns toward me, her eyes wide. Then, she smiles weakly, like she's nervous. "Well, of course it is. This is your house, right? 1194 Flamingo Lane."

"Uh, no. That's the house next door."

"*Gobdrops and fruitcake!*" she hisses, leaping around me to reclaim the singular present under the tree. "I thought I'd finally gotten a handle on the sleigh. It's so finicky. I swear, it practically has a mind of its own sometimes."

Thudding sounds on the roof once more, but this time, it's louder. It sounds like an entire football team is stomping around up there, every cleat in sync. And bells—I hear dozens of musical bells jingling above our heads.

"Don't you dare get them riled up, Rudolf," she shouts.

But the thudding only gets louder, and then the noise starts moving across the roof. Something heavy is being dragged over the shingles.

"Oh, no," she whines, raking her hands all over her torso as if feeling for a bulge, searching for something that should have been there but isn't. Her chest rises and falls rapidly as she gasps for air. She runs toward the window I didn't realize had been opened and screeches at the top of her lungs, "*Stop! I don't have it. Do you hear me? I don't have it!*"

The noise lifts away from the roof. Only the bells continue. *Ting, ting, ting, ting.* They shift wildly above the house, coming from one side and then the other.

My intruder sprints out of the living room. Her footsteps pound down the hallway, fading as she rips the front door open and exits the house. I don't know what comes over me, but I rise to my own feet and quickly follow her out, pausing on the threshold of the front door when I see a *fucking sleigh* flying through the air.

And a full team of reindeer driving it.

Either I'm seriously concussed and hallucinating, or the woman waving her hands above her head as she jumps up and down on my mother's front yard is exactly who she looks like.

I'm leaning toward the concussion or a really weird cheese dream.

The dream could be worse, though, I suppose. She could have been an old, beardy man.

The reindeer ignore her screams, winding playfully through the sky before aligning once more and rocketing towards a bright star next to the moon. That star pulses, expanding as it swallows the sleigh whole. Then, it winks out, dulling to the same size and glow of the stars around it.

I return my gaze to Santa.

Her arms drop heavily to her sides, and she stares open-mouthed at that distant star. She shakes her head, starting to pace the front lawn, and then she's hyperventilating and rubbing at her chest, mumbling to herself, her words too quiet for me to hear.

Santa is having a panic attack on my mother's front lawn.

I'm not doing much better, but I cross the yard with wobbly legs. "Hey. Take a deep breath."

She shakes her head again. "I can't believe this is happening. My first Christmas, and everything is already falling apart. What am I supposed to do? All those children—they're counting on me, and I'm failing them. I can't breathe. My chest *hurts*." She scratches at her chest and I quickly intercede, pulling her hands away before her nails score their way right through to her heart.

I have first-hand experience with panic attacks. They make me feel like I'm dying when I have one, swelling my throat and tightening my chest. Considering her reaction, I'm guessing this is her first ever, and I can't help but feel for her.

I step in front of her and grab her shoulders, and her pretty blue eyes meet mine.

"Take a deep breath," I repeat.

"What if my heart gives out?" She gasps, fear gathering in her eyes.

I shake my head. "It won't. I've got you. Just *breathe*."

She fights for one, and as she breathes out, I tell her to do it again. She does. I count with her. Inhale four. Hold. Exhale four. Hold. On the third try, she finally manages to fill her lungs all the way.

"Good," I say on my own exhale. "Are you okay?"

"Yeah, I guess so," she mutters, trembling, craning her neck to gaze at the pulsing star again with a grimace. "As okay as I can be after losing my father's sleigh."

I realize I'm still holding her shoulders, so I release her and clear my throat.

"Well," I start, biting my lips as my management brain kicks into gear. "I'm sure if you call him and tell him what happened, he'll understand. No one ever gets their job exactly right on the first day. I'm sure he can help you find it, right?"

I'm completely cracked to be indulging in any of this, but the poor girl is crying and her ride flew off, and I'm finding it really hard to keep being angry at her.

Just being within her orbit is doing things to me. I kissed her *boots*, for fuck's sake.

Maybe her crazy is contagious.

Her jaw clenches. "He's dead."

My thoughts screech to a halt, and I wish I could take back every word that just left my mouth. "I'm sorry," I whisper.

That's really all I can think to say.

Her dad is dead, and if that was his sleigh, I can only assume he was the last Santa Claus. This must be her first year taking over deliveries—which explains her...technical difficulties.

Her chin trembles and she bites her lower lip.

What a turn this dream took. One moment, I'm kissing Santa's boots, and the next, I feel this irresistible need to comfort her, to help her. She's having a shittier night than I am.

"Okay," I continue. "Maybe we can find it ourselves. Unless the reindeer fled to Canada or some other country, in which case, I don't think I'll be much help. I don't have a passport."

My attempt at humor earns me a small grin.

"No, I—I think they're close by. I can sense it." Her eyes

drop to the collar of my thin tank top, and my stomach flips before I realize she's not really looking at my body. Her eyes are glazing over. She's somewhere else entirely. "They're flying over a small town, circling a group of large brick buildings. I think it might be a school. A really big one."

"The university!" I exclaim with an encouraging smile. "It's the next town over."

She sighs, backing up a step as she rubs her forehead with one hand. "How am I going to walk that far with enough time to spare?"

"Borrow my car."

Her hand drops away from her face, her eyebrows rising in surprise. "What, really? You'd be okay with that?"

"Well, it's my mom's car technically, but sure." Why the fuck not, right? If this is just a dream, then none of this is real anyway. And if it *is* real, then there's not a soul in the world who would object to helping Santa.

I'm not a total Scrooge yet.

Santa sniffles once then wipes her nose on the sleeve of that red coat. Her stare is unnerving, like she's staring straight through my body into my soul. After a moment, she nods gently. "I see you now. Your name is Nicole Strobe. You're 29 years old. You stopped believing in Santa when you were seven years old, and this year, you've been naughty." My chest prickles as her eyes flick toward the side of the house, where all my mother's crushed ornaments lie. "*Very* naughty."

There's nothing I can say to that. She's right. I gaze hopelessly at the mess. "Believe me, I know."

"Maybe we can make it right together."

"What do you mean?" I ask, squinting at her.

She shrugs. "This might shock you, but I've never driven a car before."

"Never?"

"There's no use for a car in the North Pole. The machinery would freeze over in a heartbeat. That's why I drive a sleigh."

"So..."

"So," she echoes, "if you would be so kind as to drive me to my sleigh, I'll replace all your mother's ornaments for you. We both get what we need."

My heart flutters. "You can do that? Every single one?"

"She'll never be able to tell the difference," she assures me, smiling brightly.

I don't even have to think about her offer. It's too good to pass up. "You have yourself a deal, lady." I eagerly extend a hand toward her.

If all of this turns out to be real, I'm the luckiest asshole in the world.

Santa takes my hand and shakes it so hard, my shoulder nearly pops out of its socket. I gasp, teetering off balance for a moment, and the woman giggles. It's the most joyful, contagious noise I've ever heard. "My name is Mistletoe Claus, but you can call me Missy."

CHAPTER 4

*Missy*

When I imagined my future as a young elfling, I never thought it would look like this.

I mean, as I got older, I definitely considered the possibility of a late-night road trip in the human realm with a woman as pretty as Nicole, but the circumstances of that fantasy were quite a bit different than the current ones.

I didn't expect to be wearing my father's coat or to be chasing after his runaway sleigh.

He always warned me not to leave the reindeer alone for too long outside of the North Pole, especially Rudolph. That pup has always been the most adventurous of the bunch.

I've been screwing up all night, mistake after mistake after mistake. The reindeer are barely listening to me. The sleigh keeps stalling out. Christmas Eve is supposed to be a night filled with magic and joy, but I'm concerned I've cursed it somehow by stepping into the Santa role. I was never supposed to be Santa, and maybe the universe knows that. It was supposed to be my father. It was supposed to be my brother...

So much for that.

Nicole shuffles out of the house with a set of keys, and I follow her to the garage door. She changed when she ran inside. Now, she's wearing a pair of dark purple leggings, a light black jacket zipped up halfway, and a pair of fuzzy pink slippers. Her messy bun has been retied, and her pale green eyes are shielded by a pair of cute, boxy glasses.

She punches in a code on the panel, and the garage door starts rolling up, revealing a small, sleek convertible. The headlights flash as she unlocks the car and starts the engine remotely, and it purrs to life.

I whistle in appreciation as I approach the passenger side. "Wow. Maxpa MX-7 Miata, with a six-cylinder 2.5-liter engine and a Soul Red Crystal finish. You can't imagine how many men have this exact car on their Christmas list."

"Yeah, well, you can thank the midlife crisis my mom had last year." Nicole opens the driver's door and drops into the seat.

"Holly of a crisis," I chuckle to myself.

When I settle into the passenger seat, I'm struck by the strangest sense of disorientation. This car is much lower to the ground than the sleigh is. It makes me feel vulnerable somehow. I shift uncomfortably, attempting to sit up as tall as I can, though that doesn't make much of a difference. I'm too short.

A woman croons through the speakers, some song about breaking up with the love of her life.

"Well, this music is far too depressing for Christmas," I mutter. As Nicole adjusts the driver's seat, I reach forward and fiddle with the radio. I flip through the presets, but I don't find what I'm looking for, so I start spinning through the other channels.

Nicole finishes with the mirrors then stares apprehensively at me as the numbers on the radio crawl upward.

At the first jangling note, I lift my hand away from the dial and smile. The joyful clash of cymbals and twinkling piano fills the small space, and someone sings *Jingle Bell Rock.* I bounce along to the beat. "There. That's much better."

Nicole pulls out of the driveway and onto the street. "You should buckle up," she mutters.

I jolt into motion, pulling the belt across my torso and clicking it into place. "Right. I always forget these contraptions have safety belts." I wiggle in my seat. "They're so constricting."

"Your sleigh doesn't have them?" she asks. "I would imagine a vehicle that flies through the sky might benefit more from them than cars."

I laugh. "On the contrary, they would be a hindrance. Flying is completely safe in the sleigh. It was built with several safety measures, and one of them adheres Santa's boots to the base. It's easier to steer the reindeer standing up."

Nicole licks her lips. "'Course it is."

"You must have a ton more questions for me. You can ask them, you know. Total transparency." At least until we get back to my sleigh. Then, I'll have to make her forget.

That's one of the Claus rules. Adults can never remember seeing us, especially the ones on the naughty list.

Up until now, the theory of that rule never really bothered me, but I never thought I'd be in a position where I would need to enforce it. I didn't expect to be here, doing deliveries and interacting with humans on Christmas Eve, and especially not so soon.

Nicole's eyes flick to me before returning to the road. "I... actually don't. I think it might be best if we just focus on getting you to your sleigh."

I melt into the seat. That's sort of disappointing. Humans are normally a curious breed, often to their own detriment. I know because I'm half-human. The other half is elf, and I thank my stars for that, for my resilient, elven heart. It's easier to keep trusting as an elf, to keep hoping for the best in the face of infinite darkness. We were born from the stars, and to them, we return. Day after day. Night after night.

"You don't have any questions?" I press. "Not even *one*? I find that hard to believe."

She sighs. "I get it, okay? You're Santa. Children beg you for presents the entire month of December and you deliver them on Christmas Eve. It's simple. All my respect to you. Your family is single-handedly responsible for a holiday that makes up 19% of total retail sales in the American market. You're the reason I have a job, so thanks. I don't need to know anything more than that, and I don't really feel like discussing how special and wonderful your job is."

"My job isn't just about presents," I argue.

"Oh yeah?" she says with a scoff. "What is Santa about, then?"

Her tone is equal parts frustration and disbelief, and it makes me want to prove her wrong. "It's about…" I scour my mind for the right words and eventually settle on, "It's about belief in a better world. In fact, most Christmas wishes aren't for physical items at all."

"Really?"

I twist in my seat to watch her. Her lips are a thin line as she focuses on the road. I let myself see past her outward appearance, past the bitterness and disappointment, to the dreams beneath. At least *that* part of my inherited magic works perfectly. Always has.

With a small smile, I say, "*Yours* wasn't."

She tosses me a glare. "I didn't ask Santa for anything."

"But you still wished for something, and so I know it. I see it. This year, the only thing *you* wanted for Christmas was your family—or some kind of family. You wanted to feel the joy of belonging again, the way you used to when you were a kid. But joy isn't something that can be given. It's something you have to create for yourself."

Nicole's hands loosen on the steering wheel as she looks over at me, her eyes glistening with anger. That's when I realize there's more light in the car than there had been a moment before. Our car is veering into the opposite lane, a truck hurtling toward us.

The driver blares their horn.

"Nicole!" Before we collide with the truck, I throw myself forward and grab the steering wheel, wrenching us back into our own lane.

Nicole falls back against her seat, both hands flying up to grasp at her chest. I have no choice but to hold the wheel as she catches her breath. She smells so good, like jasmine and candied strawberries. My gaze is locked on the road, but when she doesn't immediately take the wheel back, I glance over my shoulder at her.

My stomach sinks when I see she's glaring at me. I don't have time to look closer. I have to keep the car on the road.

"You have no right to say something like that to me," she says in a throaty whisper. "We met approximately thirty seconds ago, and the last I looked, this car isn't my therapist's office. Where do you get off?"

I scoff. "Hopefully not here. You're driving us into another car because you're angry with me?"

Her hands finally return to the wheel, and I back off before I can be tempted to take a second whiff. She might smell pretty, but her resentment does *not*.

Nicole takes a deep breath, shaking her head. "I'm not

*angry*—I'm just... Does it even matter?" She chuckles with a bitter edge. " If we crashed, the worst that could happen is I'd wake up. You're just delaying the inevitable."

My brow furrows. "Wait, you think this is a dream?"

"Isn't it?"

I did not wind up at the wrong house, lose my father's sleigh, and partner up with a woman on the *naughty list* for her to think this is all a dream. This is real. I can't afford for her to unknowingly sabotage Christmas any more than I already have.

Reaching over, I pinch Nicole's arm.

She recoils with a yelp, and the car swerves again before straightening back on the road. She narrows her eyes at me as she shouts, "I thought you didn't want us to crash? Pinching the driver is a damn-near perfect way to make that happen."

"I was just trying to prove a point."

"*What* point?"

"Feeling pain means you're awake," I say with a grimace. "It means you're alive and that the thing that caused you pain was *real*. I'm real, Nicole, and my father was real too. You dishonor us both by believing this is only a dream."

Nicole stares at the road, the anger in her face slowly fading. "What happened to him?" she asks softly.

Turning my head, I stare out the window at the passing city lights. I will her to let it go, but of course, she doesn't. Not only have I just proven that she isn't dreaming, but now, my life probably seems a holly of a lot more interesting to her.

"How did he die?" she asks as if she needed to clarify.

"I don't want to talk about that."

"Seriously?" Nicole presses, though her voice is entirely gentle. "You just told me, in no uncertain terms, that *I* am the source of my own unhappiness."

I sigh. "That's not what I meant."

She continues, "It just seems a little hypocritical for you to shut down when you expect *me* to open up to you about *my* family. I'm not judging anything. I don't even have naughty or nice lists to place anyone on, so you know—safe place and all that."

I don't exactly appreciate what she's insinuating: that Santa is some judgmental figure who forsakes troubled kids on Christmas Eve. In reality, it's quite the opposite. Kids don't make the naughty list so easily. It's all a matter of faith, truly. There are presents in my father's bag for all of them, and there's a deep sense of joy in delivering to them, to those who need Christmas the most.

But she might be on to something about talking it out.

If I'm wiping her memory by the end of the night, why not open up to her? I don't have anyone to talk to except for the elves, and I've hesitated there too. They're mourning my father's passing; it didn't feel right to unload on them so close to Christmas. It's actually sort of nice to be asked about him. No one back home talks about him around me. They're afraid to. They treat me like I might shatter and collapse if they even say his name.

But I don't want to avoid his name.

I want to hear it. I want to say it. *Papa.*

Besides, talking about how hard the past month has been for me might help Nicole open up in return. Maybe I can get her off the naughty list.

"It was a heart attack," I admit.

The car falls silent. Well, except for the jolly Christmas music, which seems both fitting and terrible at the same time. I wait for Nicole to say something, but when I glance at her, she's solemnly gazing out at the dark road.

I fill the emptiness by saying, "Isn't that the most ironic bullshingles you've ever heard? Santa, dying of a heart attack."

She frowns. "I'm sorry, Missy."

"Yeah, so am I," I murmur. "And I'm messing up everything he worked for in one night, everything *his* father worked for. I was never supposed to be here, to be doing this. That's pretty obvious now, isn't it?"

Nicole's eyes flick to mine, and then she looks me up and down before shrugging. "I don't know. I think you look good in red."

My face warms.

"Thanks." I look down at my suit and pick a fleck of lint off the sleeve. "This is his. The elves wanted to hem it for me, but I just...couldn't let them do it. It's exactly the same, which is nothing short of a miracle. Everything else is so different now. Everything feels different, everything except for this coat. Now it's getting all dirty, and I'm sort of regretting my decision to keep it like this. It must sound so silly. Not wanting to alter it, I mean."

"I don't think that's silly at all. I think it's sweet."

Her words comfort me, make me feel a little stronger, a little braver. "It makes me feel like he's close by, like he's with me."

Nicole nods. "Maybe he still is."

"I hope so," I reply. "He's the only person who can help me turn this night around."

Her brow furrows, and there's a long pause before she asks, "You had to know this was coming at some point, though, right?"

My spine prickles, and I sit up a little straighter. "I can assure you, not a single person in the North Pole saw this coming."

Nicole winces. "I don't mean—shit, I'm sorry. I didn't mean the heart attack. I just meant, you know, the succession." She waves a hand in my direction. "You had to have been prepared to take over for him someday if you're his daughter."

The reminder makes me laugh, but it's a rather helpless little noise as I relax in my seat. "Not even a little bit. I have an older brother, Christopher Claus, the eleventh in a long line of male heirs to the Santa title. Little did *I* know, my brother had zero interest in taking up my father's mantle. He left the North Pole a month ago without a word of warning. Called me from an airport in the Caribbean to let me know the job was mine—permanently. It didn't leave me a whole lot of time to learn the ropes, hence the disaster this night turned out to be."

"That's a lot of pressure for you to be under."

"Yeah, well, I'm a Claus. We're built for it."

Nicole purses her lips. "Is it what you *want*, though? Do you want to be Santa Claus?"

I think about that for a moment. I think back on my childhood, how great it was to grow up in the North Pole, surrounded by all that light and joy and snow. Tears prick my eyes. "I love the North Pole," I tell her. "I love Christmas and the snow and the elves. And I've always admired my father's work. I think I spent more time in his workshop than I did any other place in the universe." I take a deep breath and wipe away a tear as it escapes down my cheek. "So, yeah, I think I do want this. I just worry I'm not cut out for it."

Silence stretches between us again, and I start to worry I've said something too vulnerable. But then, Nicole shakes her head. "Don't overthink it. Passion for your work is half the battle," she says. "Everything else is just...practice."

I turn to look out the window as we drive into town, hiding how much her words meant to me.

The houses glitter with so many colors, and the sky is so dark beyond them. This town is too populated to see the stars. "It might not snow here, but look at all the Christmas lights," I whisper. "They're so bright. I love getting to see them this clearly, don't you?"

Nicole peers out the windows, her head turning as she takes it all in, and a small, shy smile stretches over her lips.

She glances over at me. "I guess I never thought about that. It is beautiful."

## CHAPTER 5
## *Nicole*

"Right here, right here!"

Missy Claus—the *real-life Miss fucking Santa Claus*—is violently shaking my arm and pointing to a driveway on my side. So actually, it's a left here. But whatever.

"Oh my God," I mutter as I pull in. "It landed in the yard of a fraternity."

This whole street seems to belong to the university, because it's infested with Greek letters and school paraphernalia. Most of the houses leading to the campus up ahead are dark, but not this one. Every window here is lit up. It looks like every student who stayed at the school over the holiday is *here*, at an absolute rager.

And to make matters worse, the reindeer have been unhitched from the sleigh.

A handful of drunk frat boys are messing with them, jingling their bells and herding them around the yard, and one is even trying to climb onto Dancer's back.

Missy spots him the same moment I do, and she growls so loud, it rumbles the entire car. "*Naughty.*"

Before we even roll to a complete stop, she throws open her door and stomps across the lawn. With a curse, I quickly park the car and chase after her. Man, she moves fast. By the time I catch up to her, she's already shoving that frat boy off the reindeer.

"Get off him, you miserable sack of coal."

He staggers back and trips on the lawn, landing hard on his back.

One of the other drunk frat guys calls to her, "Hey! Chill out, lady."

Missy spouts a dangerous laugh. "Chill out? You want me to chill out? These are *my* reindeer. You shouldn't have taken them off the sleigh!" She gestures toward the sleigh, but then she does a double take, and her mouth pops open. "Where is my bag of presents?"

She turns back to the frat boy in front of her and stalks toward him, her eyes throwing daggers. "*Where is my bag of presents?*" she screeches.

The entire night sky halts to listen to her. The yard falls quiet and still, and for a few fleeting heartbeats, I wonder if she stopped time somehow.

The frat boy recovers before I do. "Crazy bitch." He starts backing away.

My blood boils at that, and before I can stop myself, I walk up to the kid who was climbing the reindeer and grab a fistful of his palm tree-covered button-up. His friends simply watch us with glossy eyes. "You're about to see an even crazier bitch if you don't answer Santa's question."

He blinks, slow and dumb.

I'm about to start shaking him when another kid steps

forward, his arms outstretched. "Hold on," he says shakily, his eyes locked on Missy. "We didn't know any of this belonged to anyone who needed it, alright? This was a mistake. The bag is inside—"

His friends spin on him with wide eyes. "Dude!"

"Would you guys shut up?" he snapped. "Do you realize we just fucked with Santa's sleigh? On Christmas Eve!"

Missy turns to look at him more closely.

He grimaces. "I'll make sure we put the reindeer back exactly the way we found them, okay? Don't worry about it." This kid doesn't look as drunk as his buddies. In fact, he looks stone-cold sober. His brown hair curls around his ears beneath a backward baseball cap.

After a moment of scrutinizing him, Missy's shoulders relax, and she steps closer with a relieved smile. "Gregory Short. 21 years old. A true believer."

He scratches the back of his neck, nervously chuckling. "Uh—yes, ma'am?"

"I'll leave your present in the house." She spins around and climbs the front steps. Just before she reaches the door, she turns back and adds, "And don't forget to call your nephews tomorrow. They miss you."

I watch his cheeks turn a deep shade of red before I follow Missy inside.

"Missy, wait up!" I weave through the sea of swaying college students, chasing the bright red Santa hat to the stairs beyond the entryway. She starts ascending the staircase without glancing back. "Where are you *going?*"

"It's up here," she calls over her shoulder. "I can tell."

*Of course, she can,* I grumble to myself as I shoulder my way up the stairs, maneuvering around no less than three horny couples. Seeing them kiss makes my skin itch. They're happy right now, but that won't last. One or both of them will eventually lose interest. That's just how love works. I guess they might as well enjoy it while they can. I just don't want to see it. Call it jealousy or bitterness or whatever. It's what I feel.

The hallway empties out on the second floor, and I can see Missy well enough to catch her arm. "Hey, can you just wait for me, please?"

Missy shakes my hand off her arm, her chest heaving. "I don't have time to wait."

She looks like she's close to another panic attack. Knowing some of what she has been through, I can understand why. That's her father's bag. Having it taken and rifled through must be painful, and there's nothing anyone can do to comfort her. She won't feel right until she has it back.

Revolving to face an open door down the hallway, she squints at it before nodding to herself. Lights shift inside and music spills out, beckoning to us. "My bag is in there."

Then, she's moving again, and all I can do is follow her.

Missy throws open the bedroom door and walks inside with so much grace and fury, my gaze can't help but wander down the length of her back. Her hands find her narrow waist as she glides to a stop just beyond the threshold. She's small and fierce, her chin raised in defiance, her little nose shimmering under the blue strip lights on the ceiling.

The overwhelming urge to walk behind her washes over me, to wrap my arms around her from behind and press my face into the side of her neck.

When my gaze finally shifts to the others in the room, my stomach flips, and I clear my head with a shake. I have no idea where that came from. She's Santa, and I was definitely just looking at her ass.

It's a nice ass.

My attraction isn't surprising. She's gorgeous, and I've had girlfriends before. No, it's the fact that I've only just met her. The sexual relationships I've had with women usually begin as friendships. We have to get close emotionally before I feel butterflies. For whatever reason, I already feel close to Missy, but maybe that's simply because she's Santa. She knows my deepest desires, my flaws. It's difficult *not* to feel close to her.

A guy sitting on the couch on the other side of the room laughs, pulling me out of my head. "Who ordered the sexy Santa-gram?" His glassy eyes rove Missy's body, and I find myself stepping closer to her.

There are five guys in this room.

Four are smiling.

Three aren't wearing shirts.

Two of them are smoking a joint.

One—the one who spoke earlier—is holding a large, red velvet bag between his knees. I want to punch his lights out at the way he keeps staring at Missy.

Her attention is centered on him, on her bag. "That's *mine.*"

He leans back in his seat, stretching his arms out over the back of the couch to draw attention to his bare chest. I roll my eyes. Stupid, drunk college boy. "See something you like, Santa?"

I'd like to shove candy canes so far into my ears, the drums rupture. His voice is so high-pitched, I wonder if his balls have even dropped. "She's talking about the *bag,*" I snap, "dumbass."

When he looks at me, it's with mild disinterest. The back of my neck prickles at the dismissal in his eyes. Most men don't see much when they look at me, even the drunk ones. I'm perfectly adequate at best, mostly ordinary and only mildly pretty. The only exceptional thing about me is my long legs.

Just look at what I'm standing next to. I'm no silver-haired fable.

"This bag?" He gestures between his legs. "Oh... This bag was found on *our* lawn. Finders keepers." Then, he turns to Missy again and jerks his chin. "You really shouldn't have lost track of your sleigh, honey, but maybe I'd do a trade."

I stomp forward. "This isn't kindergarten. Just hand it over."

Missy throws an arm out and pushes me behind her. "It's okay, Nicole." My gaze snaps to hers in surprise, but she's wearing an impish smirk. "He wants to keep my presents. So we'll just have to wait patiently and see how attached he is to them once they start misbehaving."

My face pinches, but before I can ask what she means, someone screams.

Every inanimate object in the room is coming to *life*.

The strip lights above us flash bright red. The toy robots glitch as one, *sparks* flying from their batteries, startling the frat boys closest to them. A jack-in-the-box explodes out of its container next to the guy holding Missy's bag, frightening him so badly that he scrambles onto the floor in front of the couch. The giant teddy bear sitting in the corner stands on its fluffy feet, the expression sewn into its face twisting into an angry frown. They close in all at once, forcing the boys into the middle of the room as a wicked breeze ruffles their hair.

I don't know how it's possible, but there's *snow* in here, billowing, dancing...*freezing*. The boys shudder as it pummels their skin.

I giggle, pressing my fingertips to my mouth as Missy smiles. Her face has that gray appearance again as her nails and teeth sharpen to points. My laughter ebbs as I watch horns sprout from the top of her head. *That's* new. Luckily, I've already been jump-scared by Santa a few times tonight, so I'm not totally shell-shocked.

The frat bros are not so lucky.

One is crying.

Two are wielding couch cushions as shields.

Three are cursing as toys bite and pound on their shins.

All four beg their frat brother to give the "cursed fucking bag" back.

"Take it, *take it*," he eventually screams, kicking the bag toward us. "Just make it stop!"

It happens in an instant. The snow melts midair. The toys topple over. Missy's dark visage falls away, and she beams as she practically skips across the room before hefting the bag over one shoulder. She keeps her head high as she retreats into the hallway.

I flip them the bird before slamming the door shut behind us.

Giggling, I follow Missy to where she stands a few doors down, leaning against the wall with the bag between her feet.

Something is wrong.

Her arms are wrapped tightly around her torso, and she's squeezing herself, trying to slow her breathing.

"What is it?" I ask. "Are you feeling alright?" Tentatively, I place a hand on her shoulder, trying to get a good look at her face.

When she lifts her head, her eyes drip with remorse. "I'm sorry," she whispers.

With a furrowed brow, I reply, "For what?"

"Subjecting you to that," she says forcefully, as if it should be obvious. "That sort of magic... It doesn't bode well for Christmas Spirit."

I laugh. "Don't be sorry. That was fucking awesome, whatever kind of magic it was."

Her eyes snap to mine. As her surprise fades, it gives way to a smile, and the heaviness in her stare lightens. "Papa used to call it his Krampus."

# CHAPTER 6

# Missy

"Wait, so you're saying Santa and Krampus are the same person?" Nicole asks as she presses in close to me. We're inching toward the staircase together. Her eyes are luminous, and her hands are waving excitedly in front of her as she continues, "Like some kind of Christmas Jekyll and Hyde?"

I grimace.

"Not *exactly*." Chuckling nervously, I shift the bag higher on my shoulder. "The Krampus is just an elf's shadow. Our moon side, so to speak. We all have one."

That's the easiest explanation I can come up with. The truth is a little more complicated.

Our kind were once stars, our spirits living amidst the darkness, and it was impossible not to take some of that dark with us when we fell. The Originals passed it down to us, and I will pass it down to my children someday, if I ever have them. Light and dark. They must exist together or not at all.

It is the gift and curse of our existence: to balance the delicate cosmos, just like life and death. Both come, both linger, and essentially, so do we. We're never to be seen but always remembered, immortalized in a passing season.

All eternal spirits like me live on in that familiar darkness: Santa Claus, Mother Earth, Maiden Spring, and so many others. Say our name. Dream of us. That's as real as we get.

We do not belong to Earth, though there are others like us who do.

"Well, whatever she is, I like her," Nicole says, shooting me a sideways smirk. "So, what now?"

My stomach sinks as we near the stairs. The moment we get back to the sleigh, I should wipe her memory. I have to. Now that I have the sleigh back, I need to get back on with the deliveries. Still, I feel sick about it. I don't know why.

The mesmerizer in my father's coat won't hurt her, but it will confuse her for a while.

She'll know nothing except that she took a late-night drive to look at all the Christmas lights and then ran out of gas next to a fraternity. That nice kid, Gregory, filled up the car's tank for her before sending her home. Simple. Nice.

This is just protocol, but I don't want to do it.

Maybe it's because she's my first "watcher" on the job. Papa talked about his first, how the kid had climbed into his bag when he wasn't watching and scared the peppermint patties out of him in the air. That kid got the sleigh ride of their life that night. I could tell that it broke Papa's heart to make the kid forget. He always insisted that the bag of presents should be kept in the sleigh after that night, but my current experience leads me to disagree.

And perhaps that's why I don't put the bag down right there in the hallway to grab the mesmerizer from Papa's coat. Perhaps that's why I decide to put it off as long as I can.

"In a moment," I reply, veering toward the open bathroom door. "I just have to use the bathroom real quick." And figure out how to pull up my big girl pants to do what needs to be done. It's not a big deal. It's just business.

If anyone could understand that, it would be Nicole.

I plan on hiding out in the bathroom for a moment to collect myself, but it turns out, I'm not the only one with that idea. The moment I step over the threshold, I hear sniffling. It's a small, muffled noise, but it definitely came from inside this room.

I don't see anyone right away. The walking space is empty, just a scuffed tile floor and a dirty toilet with the seat flipped up. They must be in the tub. The white shower curtain is covering it. If I squint, I can just make out the outline of a petite body.

"Hello?" I call. "Is someone in there?"

Nicole is at my side in an instant. "What's going on?"

"I think someone is crying in the bathtub."

"Well, that's not a surprise. It's a fraternity."

The person in the tub sniffles again. "No one is crying," they mutter. "Go away."

Nicole chuckles. "Right, well, now I'm convinced. It must be a ghost."

I tug the shower curtain open and find a young woman glaring at us. Her face is red and splotchy around the eyes, her cheeks wet. She has been drinking, but not in excess from what I can tell. She's just sad.

With a sigh, I drop the bag of presents and crouch next to the tub.

The girl's gaze anchors in mine, and my mind starts spinning with information. "Annie Travis. What are you doing here on Christmas Eve?"

Fresh tears well in her eyes. "Who are you?"

"You know who I am." I smile at her and flick the bell on

the end of my hat. "This just happens to be the first time we've met."

She blinks a few times, her eyebrows furrowing. "I'm not drunk enough for this."

"You're drunk enough to be crying in this gross bathroom," Nicole interjects sharply, leaning her shoulder against the wall next to the tub. Her eyes flick between me and Annie, and I'm surprised to see there's something strange and dark simmering in them.

"I'm not drunk," Annie mumbles, staring emptily at her knees.

"Of course, you aren't," I reassure her. "You're a good girl, always have been."

Annie's eyes shift to mine, and some of her defensiveness falls away. "I don't even like drinking. It's so dumb. It doesn't even feel good."

Nicole scoffs and pushes off the wall to cross her arms. When I glance up, I see her face is flushed, and her gaze flits around the room, like she's trying to avoid looking at us. I'm not sure why. Did I say something to upset her?

I turn back to Annie.

"You were crying about something," I remind her. "So, I'll ask again: what are you doing here? Shouldn't you be in Los Angeles right now?"

There's no hesitation this time. Annie covers her face with her hands and wails into them. "I *suck*. I failed a class. I can't go home and tell my parents. They'll be so disappointed in me."

I reach out and touch her arm. "Oh, I'm sure that's not true."

"It is!" she insists, dropping her hands and squinting through her tears. "Do you know how much college costs these days? They took out a second mortgage for me, and I'm wasting it."

Nicole chuckles to herself. "Now it's all making sense."

How can she be so cold? Logically, I know she's on the naughty list, but not many naughty-listers would help Santa even if they knew I was real. They would lie to themselves before believing in someone like me. My heart wants to believe the best in her, but now, I'm wondering if it's too far buried to retrieve.

I ignore her and focus on the good girl in front of me. "Your parents love you, Annie, even when you fail."

"Don't get her hopes up, Santa." Nicole's tone is caustic and gloomy. A rain cloud hovering overhead. When I throw a glare at her over my shoulder, she pointedly avoids my gaze, which is probably for the best. My claws are ready to come out.

"Excuse you, Nicole. They *do*."

Nicole rolls her eyes.

I return my gaze to Annie. "Your parents miss you," I tell her, squeezing her arm. "And they care more about you being home for Christmas than they do about you failing one class. You got exceptional marks in all your other classes this semester, didn't you?"

"Well, yes," she blubbers.

"You see?" I say with an encouraging smile. "This is just a little hiccup. Life is full of them. Don't push people away just because you're afraid of causing them pain. Pain is a part of living and loving. All you can do is keep trying." I reach into my father's coat pocket. Magic tickles at my fingertips as I withdraw the plane ticket and extend it towards Annie. "Let the love in where you hurt the most."

Annie's eyes widen as she reads the paper in my hand. Tentatively, she takes it.

"That's a good girl," I praise her.

Nicole scoffs.

That's it. My patience with this woman has officially run

out. I get to my feet and spin around to face her, lifting the sack of presents up off the floor. "Can I talk to you in the hallway?" I growl. Without waiting for a response, I stomp into the hallway and wait for her to join me.

When she exits the bathroom, I lean over and wrench the door shut before I turn on her.

"Where did this horrible attitude come from?" I demand.

She crosses her arms like a petulant teen. "I can't believe you told that girl to go home for Christmas. You don't even know her."

"I do know her," I argue. "She wanted to go home. She's just scared."

Nicoles huffs an acrid laugh. "It's not true, you know. We're all just strapped together in this rickety old rollercoaster, hurtling through life with a rush of adrenaline and terror, but pretty soon, we come down. And that's when we realize exactly how fucked up it all is. Families are broken. All of them. If you need approval from your parents to be truly happy, then you've already failed yourself."

I fall back a step, my jaw slackening.

She's extremely unhappy at the moment, and now I realize that my conversation with Annie in the bathroom set her off. She can't handle anyone finding contentment in their family right now. But that's her problem, not mine.

"Are you talking about *her*," I say evenly, "or are you talking about yourself? Because if I'm not mistaken—and I *know* I'm not—you wanted to be home for Christmas too. The only difference between you and her is that she still has one."

Nicole flinches, and I almost regret it. *Almost.*

But then she says, "It doesn't even matter. Look at *you*. You have the entire North Pole behind you, but you're still alone. On Christmas Eve. Fighting against your own shortcomings for the sake of a joy you can't even feel anymore. Don't think I didn't notice. You're not happy. This whole Santa thing is just a mask. There's no one waiting up for you, no one to make proud. You're as alone as I am. And trust me when I say, sometimes, life is easier that way."

I know she's projecting, that it's not personal, but I can't stop myself from taking it that way.

Her words are harsh, but they're also true. I *am* alone. I'll be alone when I return to the North Pole. The elves have Christmas Day off to celebrate and be with their families, so the workshop and the house will be empty. Half of my family is dead, and the other half left me behind. My brother is Holly-knows-where. My younger sister is at some boarding school for the magically gifted for at least another two years. And no one wants a griever sitting at their table.

I battle the urge to shift back into my Krampus.

I didn't do anything to deserve the way she's talking to me right now, but that's the problem with humans. They always crush the things they don't understand, like little bugs who wander too close to their feet. *This* little bug is poisonous, though.

I step forward, but the anger I feel is already slipping through my fingers.

Tomorrow is the first Christmas without Papa, and I'm so scared it's not going to feel like Christmas without him. I'm already direly behind on delivering presents. Chances are, I'm not going to make it. Not on my own. I have to accept that.

I can't make my father proud. The humans don't appreciate the legacy he created, the legacy I'm trying so damn hard to keep alive. Sooner or later, the harvestable magic of this planet, the magic that feeds the North Pole and its electric atmosphere —that elusive *"Christmas Cheer"*—will run out, and we'll have to move on anyway. A new galaxy. A new Earth.

Why not give up on this one now?

I can't feel the joy anymore. Maybe I should be a little bit naughty too.

"Maybe you're right," I mutter. I shove the present sack into Nicole's chest, and she rocks back on her heels at the impact, wrapping her arms around it with a bewildered frown. I shuck off my father's coat and drape it over the bag. "There. Keep those things safe for me. I'll pick them up from your house in the morning."

As I stalk towards the staircase, Nicole finally comes to her senses.

"Wait, what?" she calls after me. "Why?"

I pause just long enough to scowl at her over my shoulder as my hand grasps the dingy wooden railing. "Because I'm a messy elfin' drunk."

# CHAPTER 7

# *Nicole*

"Missy!"

I stumble my way down the staircase, which is made more difficult by the bag and coat piled in my arms. Those couples in the hallway are practically half-naked now. I swear, there's more slobber on their skin than clothes.

Growling in frustration, I try to track Missy as she merges with the crowd on the main floor, but by the time I hit the bottom of the staircase, I've lost her. I stagger blindly in the direction she disappeared. The crowd pushes me back and forth, and I'm given glare after scathing glare as I shove my way through the living room. Thank fuck I'm tall enough to see over most of the students, or I'd be totally disoriented.

I go to shout her name again, but the sound catches in my throat when I see her stepping up onto the coffee table, a vodka bottle raised in one hand.

"LET'S PARTY, GRINCHES!" she yells, smiling as she throws her head back and chugs straight from the bottle. The party surges, cheering and drinking around us, invigorated by her energy. It's impossible *not* to feel it.

Her magnetism.

Even *I'm* stunned by it for a moment, by how beautiful she looks, how her hair shimmers like tinsel under the energy-saving bulbs. She pushed the sleeves of her tight red shirt up, and now I can see the skin beneath them. Her forearms are covered in colorful tattoos: inked strings of cranberries and popcorn, shining stars and Christmas lights, and an incredibly intricate snow leopard. Just based on what I can see, I'm guessing the tattoos continue all the way up her arms. It makes me wonder exactly how much of her is decorated like that.

Who the hell is this chick?

Well, other than *Santa Claus*, obviously...and a goddamn work of art.

I walk in a daze up to the coffee table and swallow my shock. Whoever she is, she can't be doing this. What about the sleigh sitting outside? What about Christmas? "Missy," I hiss.

"I can't *hear youuuuu*," she sings, closing her eyes as she sways to the techno music. Then, she spins to the DJ in the corner and shouts, "Turn it up!"

The guy smiles and bobs his head as he obliges her request.

The whole room seems to shudder as the beat intensifies. I'm knocked into from every direction. I grip the bag a little tighter, trying my hardest not to let it be jostled right out of my hands. There's not enough room to breathe anymore. Everyone is trying to get closer to Missy, and I don't do well with crowds. Some people like this kind of thing. For me, it's suffocating. Every brush of their bodies burns through my clothes and sear my skin. The more movement, the more it burns.

I don't want to leave Missy here like this, though, so I stubbornly remain in the same spot, letting the crowd continue to bruise my arms.

I call her name again, but she doesn't hear me. Missy is tugging an older female student up onto the coffee table beside her, dancing against her back as she tilts the mouth of the vodka bottle between her new friend's lips. Those bright blue eyes turn to slivers as Missy gazes admiringly at the girl.

My stomach drops, and I suddenly want to rip the crawling skin from my bones.

After a moment, I realize it's *anger* burning through my veins, hot and sticky and impossible to ignore. I want to scream. I want to rage. I want to punt that pretty college student right off these premises, so hard that she would feel the imprint of my foot on her ass for days.

*I* am the one here with Santa.

*I* am the one helping her save Christmas.

If anyone deserves to dance with that beautiful creature, it's *me*.

But I have no right to feel possessive over Missy, do I? I shouldn't feel as if she owes me something, because she doesn't.

Gritting my teeth, I retreat to the front of the house. There are fewer people here, seeing as the living room is the place to be. The couples on the staircase are gone. As my skin settles and the heat in my blood fades, I look over my shoulder, watching Missy bounce on the balls of her feet and pour liquor into some brunette's mouth.

The air steals out of my chest again.

Why am I bothering with any of this? She doesn't need me. *No one* needs me. It's not my responsibility to save Christmas, and it's certainly not my job to watch over Santa in some horny frat house when she refuses to leave.

Let her party. Let her forget about Christmas.

Before I can lose my nerve, I kick the front door open and step into the tepid night air. I stalk over to the sleigh, the team of reindeer re-hitched in front of it.

The yard has mostly cleared out, but there's one guy passed out cold in the center, his even breathing the only thing assuring me he's alive. Good List Gregory is out here too, petting the reindeer at the front of the herd. I can't see the animal's nameplate around GLG's body, but I'm assuming that one is Rudolf—its nose is shining a bizarre, undulating red.

Go figure. I wonder how many other absurd Christmas tales are true. Not that I actually want to know; I've had more than enough education for one night.

"Hey," GLG greets me as I approach the sleigh. "Where's Santa?"

"Tongue deep in some college chick's mouth by now, probably," I mumble under my breath. The words are reactionary, charged by the emotions I felt as I watched Missy comfort that girl in the bathroom and as she danced with that student on the coffee table.

I'm overcome by very strange, very unwarranted pangs of jealousy.

Which is ridiculous.

I don't even know if she likes girls like that.

The way she smiled at me after I kissed her boots earlier tonight has filled my head with all kinds of wild ideas. Call me crazy, but getting on my knees for her made me feel special. Now, I just feel dumb. I don't like the thought of her making anyone else do that. Kiss her, that is, even if it's just her boots.

I drove her here, nearly crashing my mom's "baby" *twice*, and she just turned around and decided to party the rest of the night. She completely brushed me off.

Considering the way we left things, I doubt I'm getting those ornaments she promised me either. So I just wasted hours of sleep and half a tank of gas for nothing.

Well...fuck her too.

GLG either didn't hear my bitter comeback, or he's as

shocked by my response as I am. He blinks at me, his brows furrowing. "What?"

I spin around to face him and bite out, "Santa's still inside. If you want to sit on her lap and tell her your secrets, or take body shots off her or something, you should probably hurry up. There's already a line."

It takes him a few beats to gather his wits enough to stumble back across the yard.

As the front door shuts behind him, I throw the load in my arms onto the velvet seat of the sleigh. I'm not going to carry around her crap for the rest of the night, illustrious Santa figure or not. I'm not doing this stranger any more favors when I can't even help myself.

I stomp over to the convertible and dig the keys out of my jacket.

But as I unlock the car, I *do* pause, because there's frost on the window. Perfect little crystalline formations trail from the car handle to the top of the glass.

There is absolutely no explanation for the frost. It's not cold outside. This is *Florida*, for fuck's sake. I press my fingertips to the glass, and a chill bites at my skin, sinking straight to the bone. I pull my hand away and scan the driveway. I stand there for a long moment, heart beating hard against my ribs. Something is off here beyond the ice; I just can't tell what it is yet. Turning slowly, I look over the property.

My gaze catches on a stream of white against the grass.

It's *ice*. More frost, like what's covering the car window, and it leads straight to the sleigh nestled against a line of flowering bushes on the other side of the yard. Frost kisses several of the low-hanging branches.

As I scrutinize the area around the sleigh, I catch a flicker of movement. I lean forward, bracing my forearms on the top of the convertible as I squint to see the activity a little better.

The movement I saw was a head of hair shifting away from the bushes. A woman with long, black hair and a navy blue cloak wrapped around her shoulders steps forward. She's thin and tall, with delicate facial features. She approaches the sleigh and kneels beside it, ducking out of sight for a few seconds. When she straightens, her eyes are trained on the items I threw onto the seat, and the smirk on her face is downright *wolfish*.

Is she going to steal them?

I skirt around the car as quickly as I can, working myself up into a brisk jog as the woman hauls herself into the sleigh. *"Hey! Get out of there!"*

The woman's head snaps up, and when her gaze lands on me, she rolls her eyes. "Oh, I thought we were free of you. What do you want?" She steps up to the edge of the sleigh, glaring down the length of her nose at me.

I amble to a stop a few feet away, breathing hard. "What do *I* want? What do *you* want? Why are you climbing into this sleigh?"

"I don't see how that's any of your business."

My eyes narrow. "Seeing that Santa asked me to keep her bag of presents safe, I think it *is* my business."

The woman scoffs. "It looked to me like you were about to abandon them altogether. That's not keeping them safe, is it? Which is just as well. You're not suited for such a responsibility. You're only human—a *skeptic*, as a matter of fact. Go on home. I can take care of things from here."

My neck prickles with heat. "And who are *you?*"

She smiles then and jumps down from the sleigh. As her feet slam into the ground, hundreds of little frost particles swirl in the air around her. "I'm Jack Frost. Missy is an old friend of mine."

*Jack Frost...*

That's where all the ice came from. My god, how many

mythological figures am I going to meet tonight? My head spins.

I see as she draws closer that Jack's hair isn't black. It's a deep, midnight blue. It's the color I imagine frozen limbs turn just before they fall off. And her eyes are the palest blue I've ever seen. She's stunningly beautiful, in a cold, nightmarish way.

"A friend?" I echo.

"Yes! Which makes me the perfect person to step in for her. I know the delivery route, the rules, and I even have magic that will help make up for all the time she wasted with *you*. You weren't helping her, you know? You're hindering her. She should have called me in the moment the reindeer spooked."

Her insult hits me first, and I bite the inside of my cheek to keep my expression under control. But then, just as quickly, I catch something peculiar in what she said.

"How do *you* know the reindeer spooked?" I ask.

Her eyes widen slightly as she realizes what she let slip. There's no way she could have known the reindeer spooked unless she had been there, on my mother's roof.

She tries to cover it up with a laugh. "Well, it's obvious, isn't it? How else would they have ended up here?"

"Right, well, Missy didn't mention you, so I think you should leave," I snipe.

Her face falls. "I don't think that's the best course of action. Someone has to deliver these presents, or Christmas will be ruined. I warned her about this. She's clearly not ready."

"But you are?"

"Of course I am," she scoffs. "I'm a high elf ruling over this season. I was *born* ready."

I squint at her. "And what exactly would you do differently?"

Jack battles a smile, but it's too sick and wild to be restrained. "Everything."

Rudolph huffs at the front of the sleigh, turning his head to stare at her. The red light emanating from his nose flares brighter, washing us both in crimson. I don't think he likes her.

Oily guilt simmers in my belly. I don't like Jack's superior tone. Missy *was* ready. She was surprisingly happy to get the job done, all things considered, and she wasn't letting the growing pains get to her. Until she met me. If anything, it was *my* bad attitude that pushed her over the edge. I know that.

It's one thing to leave her stuff here. It's another thing entirely to let someone else replace her for the rest of the night without her knowing. And besides...that's her father's coat.

I don't trust this woman to pick up the slack out of the goodness of her heart. She has ulterior motives. She might even be partially responsible for the difficulties Missy had tonight. Who knows what she'll do to Christmas if she gets her hands on it.

I'm the only one here to stop her. I'm the only one who can make it right.

So, I lift my chin and declare, "Missy will be delivering the rest of the presents tonight, so you can go."

"When? I don't see her."

"She's going to do it," I say more forcefully. "I'll make sure of it. The sleigh will be back on the road—er, in the sky—in no time."

"You really think you can manage that?" Jack sneers.

"I think I'll manage just fine. Toy distribution is my job, actually."

Jack purses her lips like she tastes something sour. "I see."

When she looks me up and down again, I can *feel* her displeasure. An icy darkness skitters over every inch of my bare skin. I ignore the menacing sensation and stalk forward, pushing past Jack to get to the sleigh. Reaching in, I snatch up the Santa coat and fold it over my arm before turning to face her again. "I have it all handled. I'm going to go get Missy now, and I think it's best if you're gone by the time we get back."

One dark eyebrow lifts in defiance as she replies, "Don't say I didn't warn you. You think you mean something to her, but you don't. You're human. At the end of the night, you won't even remember her."

I hesitate. "What are talking about?"

Jack shrugs. "Ask her. Or don't. It won't matter. Tonight will end in disaster without me, but go ahead and have fun playing Santa's helper while you still can."

With a smirk, she draws one side of her cloak up and around her, and the air shimmers with sparkling frost, drawing inward as she disappears from the center. That airborne frost forms a star of ice and then bursts in a controlled flurry of snow. As the particles disperse, they evaporate.

It was like she was never even here.

But she *was* here, and now I have no choice but to retrieve Missy from that frat house and somehow persuade her to fulfill her duty.

# CHAPTER 8
## *Missy*

I swing my hips to the beat of the rock song, my head buzzing and my body tingling from that last shot of vodka. I've had, arguably, way too much, but my brain is in no condition to regret it and scold me...yet.

The goal is to get so drunk, I can't remember why I needed to. I think it's working.

Another college guy tries to wiggle up next to me, and I quickly spin so the bell of my hat slaps him across the face. He hisses, staggering away, and I smile. I don't feel like talking to anyone. If we talk, I'm going to see them. Every bit of them. Who they are and what they want, what they *need*. I just don't have room for it right now. I don't have the strength to bear it the way my father did, all that knowledge and hope.

They don't even appreciate what we do—these selfish humans.

A warm hand wraps around my upper arm, and I spin around, fully prepared to wield my heavy bell against the newcomer, but I look up at a pair of familiar green eyes.

"Nicole! You're back." My words are a little slurred.

Her gaze tracks across my face, and she frowns as her hand tightens on my arm. "Missy, we have to go."

She tries to tug me toward the door, but I dig in my heels and resist.

"But I love this song," I whine.

Nicole makes an exasperated noise somewhere between a sigh and a growl. When I pull away, she crosses her arms and says, "Do you even know what this song is about?" She's referring to the barely-veiled hedonistic lyrics blaring all around us.

I laugh. "I might be Santa, but I'm no saint. I had a life before this, you know? I loved parties. I was *wild.*" I roll my hips, letting my head loll back as I surrender again to the beat.

When my eyes open, I see Nicole is watching me intently, her lips parted and jaw slack.

"Why does that shock you?" I ask, drawing closer to her as my voice drops to a whisper. "You don't think us Clauses know how to be naughty? I'll have you know, I'm the *naughtiest.*"

I press against her, chest to chest, and rest my forearms on her shoulders.

Her brow furrows behind the frame of her boxy glasses, but her lips twitch in the beginnings of a smile. "You are the drunkest, at the very least."

"Oh," I sigh, pouting as I lean my weight against her. She's so tall. "I don't know about that. My brother might have me beat on that front. On all fronts, if I'm being totally honest. But he's had more practice."

Nicole's eyes soften. "I really need to talk to you. Let's go outside."

I pull away. "I don't want to talk. I want to dance."

"Missy, listen to me. This is important. This is about Christmas."

"That's what I've been doing this whole time—*thinking about Christmas*—and look at where it got me," I argue. "Look at where it got my father. Clearly, I'm better off staying far, far away from Christmas. At least I'm appreciated around here."

I gesture to the party around us.

Nicole rubs her forehead, and that's when I realize she has my father's coat folded over her arm. She must have left the bag outside. "Missy, you're Santa Claus. Millions of children all around the world appreciate you. They *adore* you." She steps forward and reaches for me, but I back away.

"Until they resent me. Until I'm nothing more than a fairy-tale they keep alive for *their* children. Here, I'm always real. I can be seen and felt." I clutch at my chest, bunching the material of my shirt in my palm, and Nicole's gaze briefly slides down to study it. I sway to the music again, but I'm not really trying. "I just want to be real again."

Nicole grabs my elbows. Her eyes flutter, and it takes her a long time to find the words to respond. "I know tonight has been hard for you," she says, "and I know I didn't make it any easier. But it's not over yet. It's not over until you stop trying. So, just give yourself one more chance to do what you love, Missy. Give *me* one more chance to help you. I can explain everything if you just come outside with me. You'll feel better afterward, I promise."

Her words tear through my drunken haze. Our eyes meet, and I see the guilt in her heart. She means it. All of it.

But I'm not ready to leave yet. I want to enjoy this side of her for as long as she allows it —the vulnerable and hopeful. She has kept it locked up for far too many years. I smile and drift forward, my body brushing against hers as I surrender to the music. "Okay, I'll come outside, but not until you *daaaance.*" My hands coast up and down her arms as I bounce along to the song, my eyebrows wiggling in an attempt to coax her into motion.

Frustration and temptation battle across her features, but

eventually, she sighs. "I guess I can't argue with that. Fine. *One dance.*"

I squeal and throw my arms around her. "Yay!"

"Don't get too excited," she says with a laugh. "I'm not much of a dancer."

"Hollybaubles!" I gasp, lowering my heels back to the ground. Dropping my hands to her hips, I press myself against her, willing her body to follow my lead. "All you have to do is feel it."

Her breath catches, her nails digging into my upper arms. She tries to imitate the roll of my hips, but her movements are staggered, confused. "Feel what?" she grumbles.

I chuckle and caress her hips soothingly.

Launching onto my toes again, I grab her shoulders to whisper in her ear, "Let the music take you without worrying about what the other people in this room are thinking. They care less about you than you think they do."

"Wow. Thanks for that reminder."

I give her a chastising look.

"Okay, okay. I get it." She stills for a moment, her brow furrowing as she listens intently to the song. Then, her eyes slide to mine. Her cheeks redden and her glasses fog up, but her shoulders loosen beneath my palms. In the next breath, she tentatively rocks her hips from side to side.

"Don't be shy," I croon, taking her hands in mine. "I don't bite. Not in *this* form, anyway."

She snorts loudly then slaps a hand over her nose and mouth in surprise, and I find it totally, absurdly adorable.

I place her hands around my waist and reach up to wrap my hands around the nape of her neck. She's warming up now. I close the space between us and curl my body around hers, wiggling and grinding against her thigh. Her motions grow bolder, my touch seeming to put her at ease. She closes her eyes, her hands tightening around my waist as she rocks her body against my hip. The closer she gets, the better it feels, the friction and warmth. We inch together until I'm sure there's no place I can't feel her. Her thigh between mine. My body in her hands. Her exhales billowing against my parted lips.

I love the way her body feels against mine. Granted, I haven't been touched like this in quite a while, and even I can admit I've neglected my sensual side recently.

But a massive part of the excitement I feel in this moment is for *her*.

Excitement for the curves beneath her jacket. The cadence of her breathing. The way the wispy hairs around her face cling to her temples as she works up a sweat. She smells so good. I want to lick every inch of her clean. I want to hear the whimpers that catch in the back of her throat. I want to hear her scream.

"There you are," I say in a smoky murmur. "I think you've found it."

Nicole laughs airily, and the sound prickles down my spine. A warm heaviness pools in my center. "Well, I've certainly found *something*."

I pull back just far enough to gaze into her pale green eyes. She looks as aroused as I feel, with dilated pupils and heavy lashes. Her glasses are too steamed up to be useful anymore, so I slide them to the top of her head and comb my fingers through her dark hair, guiding the flyaways toward her bun. "Something good?"

Her head tilts as she considers the question, considers *me*. In a soft voice, she says, "Something...worthwhile."

Tiny electrical shocks tingle throughout my torso and into my limbs. We're pressed together as firmly as we can be, but it's not close enough. It won't be enough until I'm inside her. Until

I'm a part of her. My body makes the decision to kiss her before my brain can catch up.

And then, my lips are on hers.

Her mouth is soft and delicious, and I can't help but devour her. She tastes like lemon and sugar. The surprised stiffness in her body quickly melts away as she kisses me back, her arms wrapping around my back to pull me in. Our bodies feverishly grind together. She moans against my mouth, and I flick her lips with my tongue, begging to be let inside. *More, more, more.*

My heart thunders so hard, I can't hear the music anymore, so when Nicole pushes me away, the silence in the room is as jarring as the sudden distance between us.

A new song starts playing, but I can't pay any mind to it. All my attention belongs to *her.*

Nicole and I stand a foot apart, staring at each other. Her eyes are large and glassy, and her hands tremble slightly as she presses them against her stomach and lips. "Oh my God," she breathes, shaking her head in bewilderment.

My heart drops into my gut, and my head starts spinning.

The alcohol churns painfully in my stomach, and my thoughts instantly sober me up. I just kissed her. A human woman, without permission...and she rightfully rejected me. Not only have I dishonored my father and all of the North Pole tonight by almost giving up on Christmas, but I then threw myself at a woman who has experienced one of the hardest years of her life. And I did it knowing *exactly* what a year like that feels like.

If this doesn't put me on the naughty list, I don't know what will. My stomach clenches, my mouth watering as I stagger back a couple of steps.

Nicole stretches a hand toward me, concern etched into her brow. "Missy? Are you okay?"

"I think I'm gonna throw up," I mutter.

Bile burns at the base of my throat, and I throw myself forward, stumbling across the living room and out the front door mere moments before I have to turn and puke over the edge of the porch. As I empty my stomach, all I can think about is the little ones all around the world who will wake up disappointed in the morning, and the one inside my heart I've already let down.

I MANAGE to stagger off the porch, falling to my hands and knees next to the house. Between heaves, I apologize to the bushes that were assailed by my vomit. I hope they don't die because of me. Bells are ringing in my ears, radiating into the back of my skull.

Has the frat house started playing Christmas music?

My body shakes all over, and my father's hat is sliding forward, dangerously close to landing in the mess I'm making. It's going to fall, and I'm too decked to catch it.

A warm hand appears on my back, and another snakes into my periphery, pulling the hat off my head. I recognize her scent immediately, floral and sweet. Nicole. She drags her hand down my spine over and over as I puke again. Her presence only makes me sicker. Her hands pull my hair back, fisting it at the back of my neck. She murmurs overhead, a string of soft words I can't quite understand as I collapse in on myself.

I want to shrivel up and die.

The only thing worse than the sickness is knowing this beautiful woman is here to witness it, that she's comforting me after I basically attacked her with my mouth.

She tells me that it's going to be okay, but I don't feel like I deserve to be okay.

When I feel like I've reached the end of the purging, I sloppily wipe my mouth on the bunched sleeve of my shirt. I'm glad I'm not wearing my father's coat anymore. I don't know if I could forgive myself if it had to bear the evidence of my failure.

"That's it," Nicole murmurs. "Do you feel better now?"

I frown, keeping my eyes closed. "I don't know."

"Do you need to throw up again?"

"No," I sigh.

"Okay. Let's try sitting up, then." Her hand finds my shoulder and gently pulls me upright.

My stomach twists a little, but I manage to swallow the urge to puke again. As I sit up, I reluctantly open my eyes.

Nicole smiles apologetically before releasing my silver hair to fall freely down my back. She scoots closer and tucks a few tendrils behind my ears. "Your hair is so pretty in the dark," she says.

I know she's just being nice, just trying to make me feel better. It's hard not to empathize with someone in misery, even when they're little more than a stranger. But that also means she must not harbor too many ill feelings about me kissing her, and for that, I'm grateful.

I lean away. "Yeah, well, at least I have one thing going for me."

Her hands fall into her lap, her thin brows pinching before she replies, "You have a hell of a lot more than that working in your favor, Missy. You have your sleigh and the reindeer. And for tonight, you have me too. I'm going to help you, okay?"

"Why would you want to help me?"

Nicole's gaze flits to the sleigh and then back to me, her eyes narrowing in determination. "Missy, I don't think this was your fault. When I was leaving earlier, I ran into Jack Frost."

My heart stops dead in my chest. "What did you just say?"

"She was trying to take over the deliveries."

My palms start clamming up. I feel damp all over, hot and

cold at once. "Jack Frost was here?" I demand, needing her to confirm it just one more time.

Nicole nods slowly, her fingers fidgeting in her lap. "She knew about the reindeer spooking. Based on the way she was acting, I think she might have been the one to do it somehow. You weren't the one who lost the sleigh. Maybe she's been following you, messing with you all night?"

Of course, she was. There's not a doubt in my mind.

"Ugh," I groan, doubling over. "That jealous *bitch*."

I turn and throw up again, needing to get this anger out. My stomach remembers my feelings for Jack as well as my mind does, and it eagerly complies, trying to rid itself of our memories. I wish it was that simple.

"Yeah," Nicole murmurs, her hands returning to my temples as she gathers my long hair away. "I had a feeling she was lying when she said you were old friends."

I glare at the pool of acid under my face.

"Friends?" I echo angrily. "No, not so much. We were a lot more *involved* before Papa died."

"Oh," Nicole exhales. After a beat, she asks, "Why is she trying to steal your job?"

I shake my head as I sit up again, pointedly avoiding Nicole's stare. "Long story."

"Yeah, well, I think we have a moment. We probably shouldn't attempt moving you too much yet. You still look a little green."

I study Nicole's face. She's smirking at me because she knows I know she's right. If I move right now, I'm going to lose the contents of my stomach again, and I don't think there's much of anything left to lose.

"Okay," I murmur, "fine. The highlights are, we dated for a year before my father died, and then she fell off the radar. She up and disappeared. No call, no letter, no explanation. It was hard enough to lose my papa, but I lost her too that day. And then, when my brother left the North Pole last month, she came back. She pretended to be worried about me, told me her family forced her to stay away and gave me all these excuses about why she couldn't be there for me when I needed her. I loved her so much, and I was so elfin' lonely that I believed them for a while. But as it turned out, she just wanted to talk me into giving up my father's job."

Nicole's lips press together, her green eyes burning with thinly-concealed rage. "Wow. Bitch is right."

I shrug. "I should have seen it coming. The Frost family has always wanted a piece of Christmas. They think it's owed to them because they're responsible for the winter season. It's not even winter for some countries when Christmas comes to town, though, you know? They're just greedy. But I think that's what made our relationship so exciting. At first, we were like...Romeo and Juliet, if you need a human comparison. Daughters of two opposing magical families. Papa tried to warn me about her many times, and I didn't listen. I should have."

The Frosts are not tethered to this planet or any other. They are nomadic elves, and they lust after Christmas and all other sources of magic they can find.

They know the power of the magic we harvest. The energy Christmas Eve exudes, the human *joy* that fills their atmosphere, is so thick and viral a presence that we can skim a few inches off the top to keep The North Pole going, to keep us returning to this galaxy year after year. In exchange, we bring them gifts. It's an old covenant, as old as the Claus name. Wherever humans are found, throughout time and space, there *we* are.

The Frosts would suck the human race dry at every turn if given the chance. They certainly try.

Nicole rests a hand on my thigh. "You couldn't have known then what you know now."

I stare at her hand for a long moment, trying to decide whether I should allow her to comfort me or if I should push her away. The way she's talking to me, the way she's touching me...it makes me want to reciprocate. It makes me want to do very naughty things to her. After a moment, I decide that doing anything at all would be a mistake, so I let her hand remain where it is.

I mutter, "No, but that doesn't make me feel any less terrible about the way things turned out."

"Yeah," she whispers. "I'm sorry."

"It's not your fault."

She gives me another meek smile and lifts the hand on my leg in an offering to help me up. "Well, what do you say we try getting back to the sleigh now and show her how wrong she is?"

"What if she's right?" I ask quietly.

Nicole rises to her knees, towering over me. "Not a chance," she says. "You're Missy Claus, remember? You are *built* for this. If your dad could see how much you love being Santa—how much you've stepped up for Christmas this year— he would be proud of you. He would be rooting for you, like I am. Believe in yourself the way he did, the way I'm sure he still does."

My heart swells. Her faith gives me faith, true or not.

I place my hand in hers and allow her to pull me to my feet. The moment I'm standing, my knees wobble, and Nicole has to catch me before I topple over. A miserable moan escapes my lips. "Oh, gingersnaps and pecan pie."

"I know," she says gently. "Come on, just a short walk, and then you can sit down again."

I lean heavily on Nicole as we cross the yard to the sleigh. My head starts spinning all over again, and it takes all my willpower not to heave. She helps me climb into the sleigh, and I collapse onto the bench. I can barely keep my eyes open.

"How am I going to deliver presents like this?" I cry, curling up with the bag of presents.

The sleigh jostles as Nicole hefts herself into it behind me. "I—uh, well, I guess I can help deliver them until you feel better. Just tell me what to do."

"I'm so tired," I whisper.

Nicole grabs my shoulders and leans down until her face is inches from mine. "Focus, Missy. Tell me what I need to do, and then you can take a nap."

I point at the dashboard installed into the front of the sleigh. "The radio," I murmur. "There's a walkie talkie that will connect you to the elves back at the North Pole. Tell them that a watcher has been given the reins. They'll know what that means."

"Yeah, but *I* don't know what that means."

Darkness tickles the edges of my vision. My bones are heavy. I muster up enough strength to say, "It means you take the reins off the hook, Nicole. You put on the coat. You drive the sleigh."

"What?" she squeaks. "I don't know how to drive a sleigh!"

"Hold on tight. The reindeer will do the rest," I mumble.

My head slackens against the seat of the sleigh. I'm still half awake, but my lips refuse to form another word. All I can do is listen to Nicole curse and mutter to herself as she climbs over me to the empty seat on the other side of the sleigh.

The reins jingle as she removes them from the hook above the radio, and I try—I really do *try*—to tell her to call the elves first, but I can't.

It's too late.

The instant the reins are in her hands, the reindeer surge forward, eager to return to work. Nicole squeals as they take off, but since the sleigh keeps moving smoothly, I know she managed to keep ahold of the reins. I'm so elfin' proud of her for that.

A melody of bells rings out as the reindeer stampede. The sleigh swings sideways as the herd turns sharply to race across the yard. They'll need as much leeway as they can get for take-off. We start to lift, just the front of the sleigh at first, but then the rest of it follows as the ancient magic hidden within the wood reawakens. It washes over me like a million feathers teasing my skin. The reindeer circle the yard in wild loops to gather momentum, rising and dipping, preparing to travel through time and space to get to the next house on our route.

Nicole makes a small, high-pitched squeak as we lift higher.

My stomach clenches, and my body turns of its own volition to the edge of the sleigh. I puke again, and the yellow acid rains down on the yard.

I hear a small, raspy male voice below us groan, and I'm able to peel my bleary eyes open for a second as we make one final sweep downward. The frat kid who was passed out in the yard is awake. Michael Dunne. On the naughty list, but not for long. "Whoa," he whines. "Aw, man, I definitely took way too many mushrooms."

Then, the sleigh veers straight up, and I slide until my back is flat against the bench. The last thing I see is streams of cobalt light as the starry night opens to envelop us.

# CHAPTER 9
## *Nicole*

Santa is a fucking *astronaut*.

I gaze in awe at the tunnel of stars and colorful galaxies swirling around the sleigh. We're surrounded by spirals of violet purple and dark pink, deep blue and green, all of it speckled with the brightest stars I've ever seen.

My hands tremble against the reins, my fingers white from twisting them in the leather. Every synchronized gallop forward nearly tugs the ropes out of my hands. We're moving faster than I expected, as if the night itself is swelling against the back of the sleigh, hurrying us along. And soon enough, the tunnel opens again.

We pass through a mouth of shimmering blue light and drop into a frigid, dark sky.

I shiver as the temperature drops, and my eyes briefly flit to Missy. She's curled up on the seat, her eyebrows furrowing as the cold washes over her. It's definitely not as freezing as it *should* be. There's a magical shield glimmering at the front of the sleigh, fending off most of the wind.

The world below is a blanket of twinkling lights. We're flying over a city.

A chiming bell rings out from the front of the sleigh, and when I glance down, I see a small screen lit up with bright blue letters. *Casper, Wyoming.*

The reindeer dive lower, and my stomach flutters as we pick up speed. My pulse quickens. Logically, I know I'm safe. My feet are anchored to the floorboards of the sleigh, held in place by more of that hard, transparent magic. Keeping the rest of my body upright is a struggle, though. Missy must have abs of steel underneath that red shirt.

That red shirt, clinging like saran wrap to her abdomen. Riding up on her hips. Revealing that colorful ink. Those cute tattoos.

I'm practically salivating, so I force the idea of her body out of my mind.

As we close in on the city, we veer toward the side closest to the mountains, where there's a little strip of houses.

The suburb is dressed up in Christmas lights and a thick layer of snow. We land on the roof of a one-story house in the middle of the subdivision, and I have to catch myself on the handrail as the sleigh slides to an abrupt stop.

Missy groans behind me, disturbed by our landing. She wiggles uncomfortably on the bench before falling back asleep.

When the shield around the sleigh falls and my ankles are released from the floorboards, I turn around and remove Santa's coat. Then, I shrug off my jacket and drape both of them over Missy's curled-up body. I remove the hat from her coat and pull it down over her elegantly pointed ears. Hopefully, that'll help her warm up while I figure out the radio.

The cold air feels nice. I forgot what snow feels like, what it smells like. I missed it.

I perch on the edge of the bench and bring my glasses down

from where they were sitting on my head. I can still feel the phantom of Missy's fingers in my hair. I shiver, and it has nothing to do with the temperature.

She kissed me. Santa Claus kissed me, and I liked it...probably more than I should have, considering how drunk she was. That's why I pushed her away, after all. It didn't feel right to touch her like that when she was half out of her mind. The moment I did push her away, though, I could tell I'd hurt her. No matter what I do tonight, I wind up hurting her.

I'm determined to change that, starting now.

A variety of knobs and buttons surround the screen, and a small walkie talkie hangs next to the rein hook. I grab it and press the button on its side. "Hello? Is anyone there?"

There's no response. In fact, there's no noise at all.

It should be making noise, shouldn't it?

I scan the dashboard again and realize there's a switch between the rein hook and the walkie holder, so I flick it on and smile when a low stream of static pours out of the walkie's speaker. I press the button again and repeat myself.

The static resumes as I release the button, and it gets louder just before a high-pitched voice answers. "Who is this?" they ask.

"Nicole Strobe. Missy told me to tell you that a watcher has the reins."

There's a long pause of static as I wait to hear back.

When the voice comes through again, it's quieter than before. "Is she gone?"

My brow furrows. *Gone?* Are they asking if she died? I guess that's not such a ridiculous question, considering the year they've had, but do they really have that little faith in her? "No, no, she's right here. She's alive. She passed out in the sleigh and is unable to deliver presents. We're at the next house now, but I'm not sure what I need to do. How do I deliver them?"

They respond instantly. "Oh, thank the stars. Okay, delivery is simple. Do you have her coat?"

I glance at Missy, now sleeping peacefully with her hands folded beneath her chin. "Yes, I have the coat."

"Perfect. Put the coat on and grab the presents you need. The coat will grant you passage into the house through the chimney or whatever vent you can find on the roof. Just leap toward it, and the magic sewn into the coat will take over. Once you've left the presents under the tree, you can return the same way you came in."

I nod, though the thought of jumping blindly into a chimney makes my skin crawl. "What about the present? How do I know which one to take?"

"The only presents you'll find in the bag are the ones you need. And before you go in, make sure you have the emergency apparition whistle with you. You'll need it if something goes wrong inside. It should be in one of the coat pockets. It's small and shaped like a candy cane, golden."

I set the walkie-talkie down and peel the coat off Missy's body with a frown. I hate the idea of leaving her out here with only my light jacket to keep her warm, but there's nothing to be done about that. Even Missy told me I would have to wear the coat.

But when I rifle through the pockets, I find nothing.

Bringing the walkie back to my lips, I say, "The whistle isn't here."

"Are you sure?"

"I'm pretty sure something like that would be difficult to miss," I retort.

Another short pause. Then, the elf replies, "Check the cookie box beneath the dash. Santa used to toss it in there by accident sometimes."

I duck to scan the hollow beneath the dash and find the box

they must be talking about. It's a small black bin filled with dozens of half-eaten cookies. I always wondered how Santa ate all those cookies in one night. I guess he—*she* doesn't.

There's a blanket rolled up beside the box, so I pull that out and lay it over Missy before returning to my search.

I shove aside a few balls covered in powdered sugar and flat butter cookies, and my fingertips finally brush against metal. I pull it out and exhale in relief. It's exactly what the elf described: a small golden candy cane with beautiful, snow-like engravings and a hole at both ends.

Sliding back up onto the seat, I inform the elf I have it.

They respond with, "You have everything you need, then. Keep that whistle with you at all times. That's the only way you'll be able to catch up with the sleigh if it takes off without you."

That explains why Missy was screaming all that nonsense back at my mother's house.

"Keep this radio on," they continue. "We'll be here if you have any further questions. Good luck, watcher."

I grimace and drag on the Santa coat. It's soft and warm in a way that only well-loved clothing is, but it does little to comfort me. I'm jumping into this job entirely unprepared, and I hate feeling like that. I like knowing all the most intimate details of a process, including the outcome, before I risk myself to the unknown. I prefer not to leave anything to chance.

My eyes drift again to Missy, and the tightness in my chest loosens. For her, I'll try my best anyway.

I grab the satiny bronze ropes of the bag and tug it open, pausing when I see the darkness inside. The outside of the bag bulges like it's full, but from this angle, it looks empty. Filling my lungs with the brisk winter air, I shove an arm in. At first, I feel nothing. But then, my hand tingles as the edge of a box prods my palm. I pull it out—a rectangular box with a bright red bow. As it emerges from the darkness, the silvery corner of another box appears beneath it, so I pull that one out too, and then the darkness closes up. It makes me wonder, for a moment, if the presents those boys back at the frat house pulled out had been cursed from the start.

As I climb down out of the sleigh, I recite the elf's instruction under my breath. "Leap into the chimney. Drop the present. Return up the chimney. This will be easy. I have a magic coat and a magic whistle. I can do this."

The closer I get to the snow-laden brick chimney, the fuller my throat feels. My heart is trying to crawl its way into my mouth.

A thousand questions whirl through my head, all the logistics. There's no smoke, so at least I know there's not a fire waiting for me, but chimneys have to be closed up when they're not in use, right? How do I get through that? What if I get stuck?

Sucking in another deep breath, I exhale slowly, forcing myself to let go of it all. Santa does this every year. The magic knows what it's doing, even if I don't.

My pulse hammers as I pause in front of the chimney.

I lean in to peer down the dark chute, but the instant I do, I feel myself being sucked into it head-first. I try to gasp, but the air is squeezed out of my lungs. Every inch of my body is being squeezed and contorted, and the edges of my vision glimmer with a faint blue light as I fall. If I hit anything, I don't feel it. The descent lasts less than a heartbeat.

Then, I'm tumbling out of the brick chimney into a warmer, brighter space.

"Ugh," I moan into the hardwood floors. "That kicked my ass."

I lift my head and look around the room. I've rolled into the middle of a cozy living room, fir garlands and twinkling lights strung all around. A tree shines with multicolored lights in front of a big bay window beside me. It's a real tree, not fake like my mom's—a stately blue spruce by the look of it. When I was a kid, before my parents split, the blue spruce was our family's favorite. There's just something about the silvery-blue needles that screams Christmas Day.

With a sigh, I push myself up and collect the presents that were pitched across the room.

I skirt an old oak coffee table to reach the tree. There's a plate of chocolate chip cookies and a glass of milk on it, plus a few papers with crayon drawings. I smile at the stick figures before placing the presents under the tree.

It's weird, being in a stranger's house on Christmas Eve, seeing all these ornaments thrown without inhibition onto the tree. I feel the warmth of the family sleeping in the other room, the love they share. Their joy is here, all around.

The smell of fresh pine fills my nostrils as I crouch beside the tree and arrange the presents behind the ones already there.

I read the names on the presents as I leave them behind: Corey and Abigail.

The tree is decorated with red and glittery gold ornaments, a few handmade from popsicle sticks and peeling craft paint. The kids here seem to be an older girl and younger boy, one with curly red hair and the other brunette. They look so familiar.

Then, it hits me like a swift punch to the gut, and I'm left gasping.

"There's no way," I whisper to myself.

Now that I'm here, I remember my sister lives in Casper. It has to be a coincidence. She has kids, though, and the fact that the sleigh traveled to this city first feels way too pointed. What are the chances?

In a daze, I stand and scan the room.

My gaze catches on the family portraits hanging on the wall behind the sofa. It's not a coincidence at all. My sister, Grace, is right there on the wall, her blue eyes staring back at me. My skin starts to feel way too warm beneath the Santa coat.

Why did the sleigh bring me here? This is some masochistic, Christmas-fueled torture.

I have to get out of here.

But as I turn to face the fireplace, I see I'm no longer alone. A little girl with knotted red hair and bleary eyes is staring at me from the mouth of the hallway. Abigail. I've only ever seen her in pictures, and not since she was three, but the resemblance to my sister is unmistakable. She has the same dimpled chin, the same strong nose we both have.

Abigail blinks a few times, and her little brow furrows as she looks me up and down. Then, she says in sleepy voice, "Aunt Nicole? Is that you?"

That just about knocks me off my feet. "You know who I am?" I whisper.

She nods, reaching up to rub the sleep out of her eyes. "You're my mommy's sister. Grandma showed us pictures of you today. She said you couldn't come to Christmas because you were busy making toys for other kids. Is that because you're Santa?"

I force a grin, even though tears prick the back of my eyes. "For tonight, I am."

"That's so cool," she breathes, a warm smile spreading across her face before it fades into a thoughtful expression. "But why can't you come back for Christmas tomorrow? You'll be done delivering presents by then, right?"

I didn't think I would ever have to do this. It was easy to keep my distance as long as my sister and her new family were only a concept, but now that her daughter is standing right in front of me, I can't fend off the viscous guilt. I used to fantasize about being an aunt. Knowing I didn't want children of my own, I'd relished the thought of spoiling them. I was going to be their favorite person. I had a lot of dreams like that, before the relationship between my sister and I evaporated.

After that, I knew it was better to stay away. Or, at least, I thought I knew.

"I don't know," I say weakly.

Abigail tilts her head. "Mommy said that too. Do you not like us?"

*No,* I want to say. *I want to love you, but sometimes, it's hard to break years' worth of silence. Sometimes, it's hard to silence your pride.*

I can't say that, though. That's a heaviness for my shoulders, not hers.

Shaking my head, I say, "I like you just fine. Go back to bed, Abigail. This is just a dream." Because it's better she thinks I'm a dream instead of Santa Claus. Missy is a far better Santa Claus than me. I start walking toward the fireplace.

"It feels real," Abigail murmurs.

I glance at her over my shoulder. "The best dreams often do. Go on, now. Get some sleep."

"I wish it was real," she says as she turns to the dark hallway. "I really want to meet you. Mommy tells the best stories about you."

I'm frozen in place, biting the inside of my cheek to keep from crying.

Abigail pads back down the hallway, her little voice muffled by the distance as she returns to her room. "Goodnight, Santa."

"Goodnight, Abigail," I whisper.

When her door closes, my whole body exhales. A sticky darkness lingers, bubbling in my belly, and I know this is exactly why the sleigh brought me here first. To meet *her.* It still feels like a special brand of torture, but perhaps a necessary one.

My sister talks about me, obviously without any sort of malice.

Abigail knew who I was instantly, and I only barely recognized her.

Approaching the fireplace, I see the photographs perched on the mantle. These are older. *Much* older. There's a picture of Mom and Grace when Grace graduated high school. Our dad holding both Abigail and Corey right after they were born. Pictures of Grace and her husband when they first started dating. And in the center, tucked between two of the rare family photos that survived our parents' split, is a picture of Grace and me.

We're so little in that picture, hugging tightly. Our grins are wide, and our hair flies wildly around our faces, electrified by the trampoline we're sitting on.

My glasses fog up as the tears finally brim over.

I lift a hand and touch the glass pane over Grace's face, but of course, it's not real enough to make me feel better. The memories of our last huge fight flash across my mind. I don't even remember what started it anymore. All I remember are the harsh words we exchanged. I called her selfish and stupid. She accused me of not having real feelings, because I guess that's my modus operandi.

I get tired and hopeless, and then I totally shut down. It's not that I don't have feelings. It's that I'm afraid to show them, or I'm not sure how.

That's the real problem, isn't it? If nobody sees what I feel, they can't reject me. They can't hurt me. But that's an extremely lonely, joyless way to live. I wish I knew how to be better. I wish I wasn't so afraid.

# CHAPTER 10

# Missy

When I wake up, there's an ache radiating through my temples and across the crown of my head. I inhale sharply and almost choke on the humidity in the air.

Sitting up, I squint at my surroundings.

The sleigh is immersed in a blanket of fog. I can only make out about a foot or so of black shingles on my side of the sleigh and the faint outline of Dasher and Prancer's hairy rumps up ahead. The screen is lit up with the city we're currently in. *Bandon, Oregon.*

Well, that explains the fog.

The last thing I remember is passing through the star portal with Nicole at the reins. Both her and my father's coat are missing from the sleigh. The sack has been left open on the bench beside me. She must be delivering presents inside the house.

My mind snaps back into place, barraging me with snippets of our conversation when I was sick in front of the frat house.

I groan, slapping a palm over my face as I melt against my seat.

Not only did I kiss that woman, but I also drunkenly poured my stomach and heart out in front of her. She had to hold my hair back. She had to listen to me talk about my *ex*. How totally embarrassing…

I can't believe Jack Frost is trying to sabotage Christmas.

Then again, she has done a lot of things lately that I never believed her capable of. A human is more supportive of me than she is, and Nicole is on the *naughty list*, for goodness sake.

I exhale shakily and grimace at the state of my breath.

Leaning forward, I dig in the bin of cookies until I find the small velvet bag containing my portable toiletries. The delivery route spans several time zones, and the only sustenance a Santa can get on Christmas Eve is milk and cookies. Carrying items to clean your teeth and face are absolutely necessary.

I withdraw my toothbrush and a Freschen fruit from the bag. I toss the bulbous blue berry into my mouth, crushing its transparent skin between my front teeth. The minty-sweet juice explodes across my tongue. I scoot to the edge of the sleigh bench and start brushing, and the tingly effects of the berry wakes me up a bit more.

By the time I'm finished with my teeth, there's a tapestry of blue speckling the frosty roof.

I retrieve my silver comb and shimmery hair powder and quickly brush the dried puke out of the ends of my hair. Nicole couldn't spare me from all of it, though I find it extraordinarily sweet that she tried.

She could have left me behind, but she stayed. She got Christmas back on track.

I don't know how I'm going to express to her how thankful I am for that, but I'll figure it out. She might be on the naughty list...but she was good to *me*. That counts for something. Caring for others always counts.

I'm flicking off the Polar radio when Nicole reappears, her warped figure shooting out of the roof vent and reforming in the center of the cloud of blue mist.

She staggers out of it with a gasp, her arms raised to steady her landing and her large eyes flicking from side to side to take inventory of her surroundings. Clearly, she has nearly fallen off a roof or two tonight. My stomach churns with a fresh wave of regret. She shouldn't be risking her life for me. She shouldn't be risking *anything*.

Nicole's eyes remain on the roof as she walks carefully to the sleigh, but then she lifts her gaze and sees me, and a smile lights up her face. "Hey. You're awake."

I nod, fronting a weak grin. "And you're delivering presents."

"I hope that's okay," she says uneasily as she climbs into the sleigh.

"I gave you the reins. Of course, it's okay."

She sits down, twisting to stare at me over the sack of presents, her arms folding comfortably over top of it. "How are you feeling?"

I shrug. "Better than before."

"Good. I was starting to worry you wouldn't wake until morning. I'm not sure I'm doing your job justice. I set off at least seven alarms and pissed off a chihuahua that wanted to eat me alive." Her cheeks are pink, and her hair is a wild mass of curls on top of her head. My father's coat fits her well; she's tall enough that the hem doesn't drag, and her shoulders are slightly broader than mine. She looks tired but beautiful.

"You look like you're doing perfectly fine," I tell her. "You even remembered to take the cookies." When her brow furrows, I nod at the snickerdoodle in her hand.

"Oh," she laughs. "Yeah. I was getting a little hungry. Thank God one house a few cities back set out empanadas, or I might have passed out right next to you. Who knew jumping into vents and driving a sleigh took that much out of someone?"

I nod in understanding. "It's a marathon."

"So what happens now?" Nicole asks. "Do you take over again?"

I think about for a moment. If I was smart, I would wipe her memory and send her back home right now. She doesn't need to stay. But for whatever reason, the idea of sending her away makes my skin itch, makes my Krampus want to surface. I'm not sure I could contribute in a positive way to the Christmas Spirit if she's not here with me.

"I'll take the reins..." I start slowly, "but you can help me deliver the rest of the presents if you want. I could use an extra set of hands. Sunrise is right around the corner."

Nicole tugs lightly on the lapel of Papa's coat. "But don't you need the coat—"

I stop her with a wave of my hand.

"Keep it for the rest of the night. Papa's hat will assist me just as well as the coat would." Her eyes anchor in mine, and it's hard to tell what she's thinking. So, I extend a hand over the sack and ask, "What do you say, Nicole? Finish this together?"

Her lips curl upward, and I decide it's the prettiest smile I've ever seen. She places her hand in mine and shakes it. "Together," she agrees.

I swallow the urge to pull her in for a hug and let go of her instead.

Her gaze dips to the uneaten snickerdoodle between us. After a moment, she breaks it in half and offers one piece to me. "Want to share?"

I reach over and take it, and we both take a bite at the same time. As the cookie crumbles in my mouth, I gag. This is *not* a snickerdoodle. I glance up and mark the mirrored look of disgust on Nicole's face. Her nose wrinkles up, and her eyebrows slant together as she lurches for the end of the sleigh to spit it out. I force myself to swallow before chucking the rest of the cookie in with the other discards.

Nicole's muffled words echo my thoughts. "That was terrible. I think whoever baked these mixed up the salt and sugar."

I chuckle. "Yeah, that happens a lot."

"Ugh, I've noticed." She sits back and wipes the side of her mouth with her hand. She carefully wipes her spit on the inside of her leggings, and I know it's because she doesn't want it to get on Papa's coat. "Why would people leave inedible cookies out?"

I scoot to the edge of the bench and sigh. "Santa isn't real to the parents, so they don't bother baking a second batch if the kids mess up the recipe."

"You poor soul," Nicole says with a solemn shake of her head.

"It's not so bad. There are some really fantastic cookies too. We've all gotta embrace the bad with the good sometimes."

Her eyes drift to the screen on the dash, and her face pinches thoughtfully.

"So," I huff as I stand. "You ready to get back into the sky?"

"Yeah. Let's just hope the rest of the cookies tonight are sweet."

I step forward and take the reins off the hook. "If they were all sweet, you'd get too used to the taste."

We've worked out an efficient pattern, thanks to Nicole's management expertise. In the suburbs, we trade off on chimney diving. One of us stays in the sleigh and pulls gifts while the other uses the apparition device to move quickly from house back to sleigh. We get so quick that the sleigh doesn't even need to land.

With apartments, we both deliver at the same time, working through building after building in half the time.

The sunrise looms just beyond the horizon, but I think we're going to make it.

After finishing the last high-density apartment in the last major city on our route, I'm beaming from the inside out. I climb into the sleigh at the same time Nicole reappears on the opposite side. Her pale green eyes are practically twinkling, and her arms are full of bread.

"I scored Hawaiian rolls at the last one. Thank God for tired parents," she informs me with a giggle. "What did you get?"

The present sack is small enough now that it fits in the footwell, so there's nothing between us as we scoot in close to one another. Our warmth bleeds together, and I can't help but lean in even closer. Our shoulders brush as she presents her winnings.

I smirk as I pull the napkin out of my jacket—well, out of the jacket she lent me. "My bounty was not as large as yours, but I *did* find your favorite."

"My favorite?" She dumps the bread rolls onto the sliver of bench between us and takes the napkin from me, eagerly unwrapping the cookie. When the mound of pale yellow dough is revealed, she lifts her gaze to my face. "How did you know lemon curd cookies were my favorite?"

It would be easy to blame it on my Santa sight, but I hesitate—because that's not how I know.

But how could I tell her the truth? How do I say that her mouth tasted like lemon when I kissed her, and that there's a small lemon-scented stain on the breast of her tank top that I only noticed when we were grinding against each other? That's how I knew.

Santa sight doesn't tell me those small, intimate details. That would be like trying to pick out a deer roaming through the forest from hundreds of miles above the Earth. Santa only sees the big stuff, and that all-concealing forest grows thicker the older a human gets. Nicole's loneliness was easy to see, a massive river cutting straight through. Her favorite cookie, on the other hand, is a delicate flower I would have had to bulldoze for. The smallness of that knowledge is what makes it intimate. That's what makes it special.

So, I tell her, "Lucky guess."

She opens her mouth to say something, but my stomach flips, and I push myself off the bench before she can speak. "It's my turn to take the reins," I announce. "You finish eating, and then we'll complete the last few stops. We're almost done."

I take the reins from the hook without waiting for a response, and the reindeer take off with a hard snap of the ropes. We lift into the air, leaving behind the flat gray roof of the apartment complex. A faint whine vibrates up into the floorboards of the sleigh. My feet slide backward, and that's when I realize the magic holding the sleigh together is weaker than it should be.

"What in the dusty snowglobes—" I tug back on the reins to slow our ascent, and the reindeer fight against my direction. They're scared. Something must have happened on the roof while Nicole and I were delivering presents. "*Whoa!*"

The reindeer slow, attempting to even out parallel to the ground, and I briefly glance back to check on Nicole.

She's grappling with the side of the sleigh, feeling the lack of protective shields as I do. She has to squint to return my gaze, even with her glasses taking the brunt of it. "What's going on?" she screams.

I don't know, but I need to figure it out.

The back of the sleigh dips as the magic holding it up threatens to give out, and Nicole screams again, only this time, I have no idea what she says. The wind is too loud. That vibration under my feet grows, shaking my bones. There's something wrong with the instruments.

The reindeer feel it too. They're veering side-to-side, panicking.

I reach back and grab Nicole by the arm, tugging her forward until she's sitting on the edge of the seat. Then, I shove the reins into her hands. "Keep them steady," I shout. "I need to get underneath the sleigh."

Her eyes bulge. "You need to *what?*"

"Don't let go," I roar before hauling myself to the end of the bench.

My blood starts to boil when I see the frost covering the side of the sleigh. Jack Frost. She was tampering with my sleigh, *again.*

A sharp wave of heat rolls over my body as my Krampus rises to the surface. It takes a great deal of effort not to pulverize the wooden railing under my palms. If I ever see her again, I'm going to wring her treacherous little neck.

I spin around and lurch toward Nicole.

To her credit, she doesn't recoil from my dark form. Her eyes only grow impossibly larger as she yells, "What's wrong?"

"*Frost,*" I growl as my claws close around the belt of my father's coat.

Before she has time to react, I pull it out of the rings and wrap the belt around my torso, tying it securely above the metal clasp. Nicole's eyes flick between me and the team of reindeer as I slide a hand into my papa's coat just beneath her breast. I feel for the interior pocket, ignoring Nicole's hitched breathing as I remove the parcel inside. I wrap the closed strings around my wrist.

Hopefully, that's all I should need.

When I return to the side of the sleigh, I hear Nicole calling after me. The wind distorts her words, but that's for best, I think. I can't afford any distractions at this moment. I lean against the edge of the sleigh and inch my way over it. I step down onto the golden foot rail on the outside of the sleigh. Then, I carefully turn around and sit down on the hardy pole runner, allowing my legs to hang between the pole and the side of the sleigh. I'm leaning back, precariously balanced, and only one of my hands is still anchored on the curved opening of the sleigh.

With my free hands, I feel along the underside, that ridge that runs along it. It's here...*somewhere.*

The sleigh rocks again, half-falling through the sky for a heartbeat before the magic fights back, regaining control. My hand slips against the opening of the sleigh, and my heart bottoms out as I nearly lose my grip completely.

As my fingertips catch on an irregular hollow under the sleigh, I exhale slowly.

The city is a sparkling stream beneath us. A long fall.

I pull the emergency hook down from underneath the carriage. Terror pulses in my throat, but I bite it back as I maneuver my hands to get a lower hold. Then, ever so slowly, I spin my body to lie flat against the runner pole, as close as I can get to the hook. I thumb the belt clasp into the emergency hook, not even daring to breathe until I hear the tell-tale click.

There. Now, I'm anchored to the sleigh...just in case, though that won't be helping me if the sleigh falls out of the sky.

I turn my upper body and pull myself halfway under the sleigh. The hook travels with me, holding my body weight as I slide through the maze of anchor wells toward the engine. I see the problem before I reach it.

There's a sheet of thick ice covering the instruments, and the gears are grinding helplessly beneath it. The faint smell of burning leather fills my nostrils. I need to fix this quickly before the belts start to snap, both the ones in the engine and the one around my waist. Keeping a tight grip on the edge of the engine cutout, I grapple with the parcel around my wrist. A chunk of porous, black matter hits me in the face and falls, but I catch the second one. Verbrennen Coal.

My father's sleigh has broken down in the freezing temperatures of Earth too many times, and he learned to always carry this in his coat. I'll have to refill the parcel when I get home.

I hate Jack for making me do this. It feels like an erasure of some precious piece of him. His hands were the last ones to touch this bag, this coal. I can't help but feel I'm diluting his touch with the presence of mine. I didn't want the coat to change, to be altered. But now, it has to be.

Darkness clouds the edges of my vision. My Krampus is in control.

As I lift the coal to my mouth, I allow the rage in my body to gather in the back of my throat and tumble out. My hot breath ignites the magic in the coal, and it crackles to life. Undulating red heat starts shedding off the black surface. It's almost too hot to bear. I hold the heat up to the frozen engine, allowing the ice to melt. As the gears start to spin freely, the engine makes a loud screech, and the sleigh drops.

My body slams flat against the engine, and I barely catch myself before my face gets sucked between two large iron gears. Instead, my father's belt gets devoured.

The screeching ebbs as the belts finally catch up with the engine, and the sleigh lifts with renewed vigor. My adrenaline is still racing as I try to wrench the belt away from the gears. I watch in horror as the leather is ripped apart, and I move swiftly to rip one end with all my might to free my body from its death strap. My upper body falls as the belt breaks, and I kick my ankles up to the back of my thighs to save myself, swinging from the back of my knees on the runner pole.

"*Missy?*"

The fact that I can hear Nicole's voice now means either the reindeer are calm enough that she was able to put the reins back on the hook, or the wind shields are back up. When I crane my back to peer up at the sleigh, I see Nicole leaning over the side, her hands still gripping the reins but her face twisted in concern.

There's a faint shimmer in the air above her. The shields are working.

I clench my stomach and bend forward, twisting to latch onto the runner pole with my hands before rolling up onto it, stomach first.

My lungs burn as I attempt to slow my breathing. The sleigh's magic might be operational again, but that won't help me until I'm back in the cab of the sleigh. So, I peel my chest away from the runner and reach for the opening of the sleigh. My fingertips catch on the outer ledge, and I work to tug my trembling body upright.

As I glance up, I see Nicole is battling with herself, inching toward the hook for the reins before leaning back towards me. But the reindeer are nowhere near calm.

"It's okay," I grunt, slowly hauling myself into the cab. "I've got it."

As I drag myself high enough to anchor my feet against the runner, I realize I *don't* have it. The runner is slick from the melted ice drenching my chest, and the heel of my boot slips off the edge. My legs fall through the slot of space above the pole runner. I'm not holding on to anything, and as I slide downward, the underside of my chin slams against the opening of the sleigh, and black spots explode across my vision.

I'm going to die.

Those words resound like twinkling bells in the back of my head, but they are silenced as two hands catch my forearms. They squeeze so tightly, I know they'll leave bruises.

I open my eyes and see Nicole hanging halfway out of the sleigh. Magic shimmers around her waist, holding her safely inside the cab as she holds on to me. We've entered the next star tunnel, and the entire universe glows around us.

Nicole's face blooms red as she tugs on my arms, and I have just enough wherewithal to latch onto the side of the sleigh.

She crawls backward, and the shield envelops more and more of her. Then, she sits up, and it starts wrapping around my wrists, then my arms, my shoulders, my back. With one final pull, the magic sucks me the rest of the way inside, and Nicole and I topple into the bench seat.

I deflate between the cushion and Nicole's body.

For one fleeting second, I let myself rest in the sense of safety I feel here, wrapped in her arms and cradled against her chest. Adrenaline wars with relief in my veins. My next exhale shakes my entire body. And that's when I realize I'm *sobbing*.

"Oh, no, no," Nicole coos. "You're okay, Missy. I've got you."

She pets my hair, and I try my best to soften my sobs. I cry against her collarbone for a few minutes, and then I linger there when I've finished. The number of times tonight this woman has seen me at my most vulnerable... There's no other person alive who has.

This is my first watcher, and I don't want to let her go. I don't want her to forget these pieces of me no one else knows.

Steeling my nerves, I peel away to return Nicole's frightened gaze. I want to take off her glasses. I want to straddle her lap and fix her lopsided bun. I want to do a lot of things, and none of them are reasonable. None of them are fair to either one of us.

"Are you okay?" she whispers.

"No," I reply truthfully. "I am in agony."

She cups my chin and trails her gaze down the length of my body. "You hit your jaw pretty hard. Did you get hurt somewhere else?"

I shake my head, and her dark brows furrow.

"No, Nicole. That isn't why I—" I pause, gasping for air my lungs won't accept. "I am in agony because all I want to do in this moment is kiss you, and I shouldn't."

Nicole is taken aback for a moment, her lips parting as she studies my face. Then, very quietly, she says, "Why shouldn't you?"

My mind stills. *Why shouldn't you?* As if she *wants* me to.

"I thought you...didn't like it? When I kissed you earlier, you pushed me away."

"I liked it just fine," she murmurs. "I just didn't like that you were drunk."

My heart starts pounding. "Oh."

The air between us electrifies, and I can't tear my eyes away from her, even as the sleigh exits the tunnel and a sky full of stars reappears around us. Nicole brushes my hair out of my face, tucking the strands behind my ear before she trails her touch down the length of my neck and over my collarbone. With one finger, she traces the edge of a tattoo on my chest that's mostly hidden.

Nicole studies the ink with a small smile, and then her lashes sweep up as she returns my stare. "How many tattoos do you have?"

I graze a hand over her hip, resting it against her waist. My skin is still gray. I'm still in my dark form, at least partially, and she wants me to *kiss* her like this? She's certainly a brave little human. I almost want to see how much braver she can be.

"I don't know," I rasp, forcing my dark form to recede. "Do you want to take my clothes off and count them for me?"

She huffs a soft laugh, and we lean in at the same time. My legs tangle with hers, my entire body yearning for her lips. I only get to savor the faintest brush of her mouth before the radio sputters to life. It startles Nicole, and she quickly spins around to look at it.

I sigh and sit up.

A familiar voice pours through the speaker. The head elf, Betty. "North Pole to Santa," she says shakily. "I repeat, North Pole to Santa. We received alerts about a malfunctioning engine. Are you okay out there?"

I grab the walkie and reply, "We're okay. I was able to fix it. Listen, I need you to send out the TWAT."

Nicole's eyebrows lift in surprise, and she bites her lower lip.

"The TWAT? Why do you require the TWAT?"

Nicole's face reddens as she fights to keep silent, laughter shaking her shoulders. A little squeak slips out that makes me want to kiss the fa-la-la-la-la out of her.

I bite the inside of my cheek to keep from smiling and inform Betty of Jack Frost's interference. After she assures me the team will be sent out immediately, I return the walkie to its holder and turn to face Nicole as she absolutely loses it.

"What the hell is a TWAT to you?" she gasps between giggles.

It's impossible not to smile as I tell her, "It's the Tenacious Watcher and Adversary Team. They're elves trained to track down and immobilize dangers to the Christmas delivery route. The TWAT will take care of Jack Frost until I have the time to deal with her."

Nicole starts laughing harder, wheezing mutely as she doubles over. "A Christmas..." she gasps, "TWAT!"

A giggle of my own bubbles up, and we both dissolve. By the time the sleigh lands on the next house, tears have streaked our cheeks, and we've wiggled so close, I can smell the creamy lemon stain on her shirt again.

# CHAPTER 11

# *Nicole*

I stare across the street at my mother's tan, one-story house, my arms wrapped tightly around my knees on the neighbor's roof as Missy delivers the last present. The present that initially led her to me.

We've come full circle.

The drop from this roof to the ground below is not the only thing that frightens me. I'm afraid of what will happen when Missy returns. Throughout the last leg of the delivery route, Jack Frost's words haunted me. She had said Missy would do something to me at the end of the night, something that would make me forget her. Now, a blanket of pink and orange is cresting the horizon; the night is nearly over.

Clearly, Jack isn't someone who can be trusted, but she made it sound like a promise.

I can't be the first person to ever meet Santa. Santa has been around for a long time, and the elves apparently have a term for us. *Watchers*. This has happened before, and yet, there is no evidence of it in the human world. I've never met or heard of anyone who has actually experienced something like this, so maybe there's some truth to Jack's warning.

I've been too afraid to ask Missy about it, too afraid it might cut our time together short.

The vent behind me begins pinging, and as I glance back, Missy walks out of the blue mist billowing around the chute. Her eyes land on me, and she raises her arms to the sky with a victorious grin. "The last present is *officially* delivered."

I lean back on my palms and offer up a bittersweet smile "Don't forgot about my mother's ornaments."

"Ah, yes," she sighs dramatically, perching her hands upon her hips. "Your *salary*. Your doubt wounds me, Nicole. I'll have you know, your mother's ornaments were restored to the tree the moment we pulled out of the driveway last night."

"Of course, they were," I say with a chuckle. "I can't believe that was only last night. So much has happened since then. It feels sort of like a dream."

Missy scoffs as she sits on the roof beside me, close enough to prod her shoulder against mine. "The alarming terror of a malfunctioning sleigh and a Krampus Claus. Real sugarplum-dream material you got there."

"Are you kidding? It was amazing."

She gives me a disbelieving look. "Sure."

"No, I mean it, Missy. I helped you deliver presents to thousands of kids. If it wasn't for you, I would have spent the night alone. I'm grateful you delivered that present to the wrong house."

She nods slowly and replies, "I'm grateful we met too. I don't think tonight would have been the same without you."

"Even though it was my fault you drank yourself sick?"

She nudges me with her shoulder again. "That was *my* fault. I've been running myself ragged getting ready for Christmas. It's been a nightmare, and the panic of my brother leaving didn't leave a lot of room for me to work through my feelings. I never imagined I would have to fill my father's shoes."

With a wry twist of her lips, she reaches forward and brushes her hand across the furry lapel of her father's coat.

I catch her hand, and her eyes snap to mine. "I think if your father could see you now, he'd be kicking himself for not training you as his heir from the start. Santa was lucky to have you for a daughter."

She threads her fingers with mine, her cheeks flushing. "I'm glad I didn't have to do it alone this year."

"I hate being alone lately too," I mutter. "My head is too full when I'm alone. I keep reliving the same handful of rotten moments from my life, over and over. The morning my dad left my mom. That fight I had with my sister before she went to college. The night my ex came home and ended a decade of my life. It's like I get trapped in that feeling, taken captive." I clutch at my stomach, wishing I could rip the bottomless chasm out to show her exactly what I feel.

But when I glance up, she's gazing at me with total and utter understanding. I don't know how she manages to convey so much in one look.

I smile sadly and whisper, "You brought me out of it tonight."

She squeezes my hand tightly. "You quiet my hurt too." That small confession makes my heart soar.

"At least I can think of *this* moment now when I'm reminded of the others. Being here with you."

Missy's eyes turn a bit glassy.

I cover the top of her hand and cradle it to my chest, trying to hold on to the warmth fizzling through my veins. It's slipping away too quickly. Before I lose my nerve, I lean forward and kiss her, sliding a hand into the hair at the nape of her neck. She welcomes me with parted lips, and I slide my tongue into her mouth.

Missy answers my desire with sudden vigor.

Her hand snakes between us and cradles my jaw. She coaxes my mouth wider as her tongue chases mine, wet and bold as it flicks across my lips and plunges between my teeth. This kiss might have started with me, but it's hers now. She's the one in control.

Krampus Claus has me wrapped around her dainty little finger.

She leans back until she's lying flat on the roof and drags me on top of her without breaking our kiss. Her legs shift beneath me until she's pressing a thigh between my legs.

I grasp her hip, sighing into her mouth, and her lips curl blissfully under mine before she kisses me again. My fingers roam over her. I can't get enough. The shingles scrape my knuckles as I slide my hands under her back and neck, but I don't care. I pull her closer, and my fingertips graze the hem of her shirt.

Her skin is so warm.

Missy's arms tighten around my neck as she bites my lower lip, and I moan as she nibbles on the seam of my mouth. Then, her hand slides into my hair, and she breaks the kiss to bury her teeth into the side of my neck.

My hips roll against her as she sucks on my skin, my center throbbing. I want her naked, and I want it now.

I trail a hand down and under the hem of her shirt.

She pushes me back and blinks at me, smiling as she traces the slope of my cheek with her fingertips. "Just let me look at you for a minute."

I remove my hands from her back and brace them on the roof to either side of her, hovering as I attempt to catch my breath. "What do I do now? How do I go home after a night like we've had, to what I had before?"

Her eyes narrow slightly. "Maybe you don't."

"What?"

"You don't have to go home right away," she whispers. "You could come with me."

"To the North Pole?"

Missy nods. "Yes, but I should warn you—it can only be for the rest of Christmas Day. If you stay any longer, you'll be stuck in the North Pole until the next Christmas Eve. Next year."

My brows pinch. "Really? Why?"

Her fingertips continue to memorize the lines on my face. "The North Pole isn't on Earth. Our stars just happen to align with Earth's on Christmas Eve. Elves can travel back and forth freely throughout the year if we have the means, but humans don't have that ability. *You* can only travel back and forth while our stars are aligned with yours."

I nod slowly, absorbing all of that. "But as long as I return to Earth by the end of Christmas Day, I'll be fine?"

"Yes, before midnight."

Well, isn't that the most Cinderella-esque deal I've ever been offered? I thought they were only fairytales.

I push myself up. "Okay. Let's go."

Her face brightens with a smile, her eyes twinkling. "You really want to come?"

"Duh," I laugh. "It's the North Pole!"

Missy leaps upright with a squeal, tugging me into a brief hug before she spins around and drags me toward the sleigh. "I have so much to show you."

We settle into the sleigh, and as she pulls the reins off the hook, I lean forward and wrap an arm around her waist. She falls back onto my lap, and I squeeze her tightly so she knows I want her to sit right here.

"I want to see everything," I tell her. "As much as possible so I don't forget it."

She glances at me over her shoulder, and I don't miss the sadness flickering like a candle in her eyes. If there's something she needs to tell me, she chooses not to.

All she says before snapping the reins is, "You got it, precious."

When we emerge from the tunnel of galaxies this time, we drop into a bone-chilling climate.

I start shivering instantly, even with the Santa coat on. Missy must be *freezing*. She doesn't show it, though. She glances back at me with a wild grin, her eyes glittering like stars. That's when I realize her gaze is actually reflecting a massive shield erected in the sky ahead of us.

We're flying towards a ginormous cylinder, and it looks like it's made of millions of rapidly falling stars. Their tails leave sparkling trails behind them, outlining the otherwise invisible barrier. Luminous orbs gather in the clouds above it, the cylinder's source. They hurtle down like angels from the heavens.

It's the most beautiful thing I've ever seen, aside from the elf beaming over her shoulder at me. She's the most beautiful thing in the universe, I'm sure of it.

My eyes burn in the cold air, but I fight the urge to blink. I don't want to miss a single second of this. The sleigh flies around the cylinder in wide circles, drawing closer and closer with each revolution. I see glimpses of a bright little city on the ground in its center. It's there. The North Pole.

Missy snaps the reins. "Zuüsten!"

I'll never get sick of hearing her speak elvish.

She's not looking at me anymore. Her entire focus has shifted to the reindeer. Rudolph's nose flares at the head of the team as we turn to face the cylinder directly.

As we near the barrier, I see the stars are burning with white fire, and fear spears through me. We have to pass through them somehow. The shields of the sleigh seem to soften the wind well enough, but anything more physical will certainly pass through, the same way Missy did.

"Uh..." I shift on the bench, my voice filled with apprehension. "Missy?"

"Hold on to something, sweet girl," she shouts over her shoulder. "This flight is about to get a little rocky." Then, she laughs wildly, manically, as the sleigh suddenly dips and we dive right through.

I clutch the back of the bench, a squeal tearing out of me as the reindeer weave between the blinding orbs. The barrier is thicker than it initially seemed. A vicious heat washes over me, and I can't breathe as I gape at the world of light that wraps around us. The stars can definitely pass through the shields. I know because they start bouncing off the outer edges of the cab. I scream when a star slams into the curved side to my left, and I scramble away. The stars don't damage the wood, to my surprise. Instead, the collision points glow a soft blue after they're hit.

Some kind of magic prevents the wood from catching fire.

Each hit rocks the sleigh from side to side, though, and I'm glad Missy told me to hold on, because I can barely keep my body from flying off the bench. The reindeer veer sharply, adjusting our trajectory as we navigate the sparkling shower. I can tell they've been highly trained for this precise purpose. Through their guidance alone, the center of the sleigh remains untouched by the burgeoning star fall.

Then, almost as quickly as we dove in, the sleigh shoots upwards, and we leave the barrier of stars behind.

The warmth of the stars is replaced with more of that brisk winter chill. Snow flutters around us. My breath puffs white in front of me as I exhale shakily and slowly loosen my death grip on the bench. I peer over the side of the sleigh as we fly in a wide arc along the mystical barrier, descending towards the city below. The North Pole is a conglomeration of quaint wooden buildings, their roofs caked with snow. All the narrow cobblestone streets between the buildings, on the other hand, are freshly plowed, and they glow with that same gentle blue hue I'm realizing is the tell-tale mark of Christmas magic.

We fly into a circular plaza with a massive clock tower and shimmering confetti scattered across the cobblestone. The barren streets fill me with apprehension.

Where is everyone? Where are the elves?

The sleigh slides to a graceful stop next to the clock tower, and I'm relieved when I see several short, slender figures run out of the buildings up ahead. I think they are the stables. The elves approaching must be reindeer handlers, wearing the loveliest velvet green suits and plush winter gear. Their furry earmuffs are larger than human ones, oblong to stretch over the very tips of their ears. They wave cheerily at Missy before unhitching the reindeer and leading them away.

I follow Missy as she climbs out of the sleigh and heads toward the clock tower.

A female elf stands there with crossed arms and a smirk. She's older than the others, though the signs are subtle; the pinkness in her cheeks is softer, there are fine lines around her eyes, and there's a dullness to her silver hair. The door at the base of the clock tower is wide open, and there's a desk beyond the threshold with radio equipment set up on it.

"Well done, my dear," she says as Missy approaches her.

Missy doesn't say a word. She simply embraces the woman like a child would a beloved relative, and the woman melts, squeezing her tightly in return.

After a long moment, the woman grips her arms and peels her away. "I mean it. You did beautifully, all things considered. Now, it is time to rest." Her eyes slide to me. "And I see you've brought the watcher back with you. I assume I do not have to warn you about what you are up against."

"No, Auntie Mags," Missy sighs. "I told her."

*Auntie.* So she *is* family, in one form or another. Mags skirts around Missy to reach me and grabs my hand, holding it gently as she says, "Thank you for what you have done for Christmas, Nicole. The fates blessed us this evening by bringing you two together, and we will not soon forget it."

She smiles weakly, and my stomach sinks. I don't like the way she said that.

Before I can work up the courage to address it, she lets go of my hand and spins to face Missy. "I've prepared some cocoa for you and your watcher. It's in the workshop. Before you go, though, you should know." Mags' gaze flicks briefly to me before she nods up at the clock tower. "TWAT secured Jack Frost, and they're waiting for your judgment. When you get a free moment."

I might have laughed at the acronym again if it wasn't for the mention of Jack.

Missy visibly recoils from the information, and a furrow digs into the flesh between her eyes. I find myself wondering when she saw Jack last. Did she still have feelings for her? Or was it just the old hurt Missy was feeling right now, revived by our current circumstances?

She sighs, gazing up at the clock tower with obvious reluctance. "I should go now and relieve the team. It's getting late."

"That sounds like a good plan to me. You would have made

your father proud tonight, Santa." Mags steps forward with a smile and pats Missy's cheek with her fingertips. "I'll see you again when the stars burst, my dear."

Missy nods, tears swimming in her eyes, and we watch in silence as Mags departs from the plaza, her form disappearing down a path leading away from town, where the pine trees crowd in to replace the buildings.

Missy's blue eyes cloud a bit as they shift to me. Her mind is far away.

"You wait here," she says weakly, inching toward the opening of the tower. "I'll be back down in a few minutes."

I surge forward and grab her arm, stopping her. "No way! I'm coming with you."

She shakes her head but allows me to hold her captive on the threshold...as if she doesn't really want me to let go. In my heart, I know she doesn't want to be alone, but she's still avoiding my stare. "You don't have to do that, Nicole. This is my mess, and I have to clean it up."

"I don't like the idea of you going up there by yourself," I insist, pulling her close. "We conquered the rest of this night together. I'm not abandoning you now."

Her gaze softens, and, in that moment, I feel completely and wholly seen. She reaches forward and cradles my face in her hands. A heart-wrenching smile dances across her lips. It makes me feel like I'm soaking up sunshine and vodka. "Okay."

Then she turns and leads me by the hand into the tower.

We leave the small communications room behind and ascend the staircase built along the circumference of the tower, up a seemingly endless spiral.

After a long few minutes of climbing, the steps end, and a dim room opens up. I realize with a start that we're surrounded by the inner workings of the clock tower, with all its gears and cogs and oiled metal. What little light there is comes from the yellow glass of the clock face across the room. The glass must be enchanted somehow, because I can't see the source of that golden light, only the soft glow it creates—and the silhouettes of three elves waiting for us.

I recognize the female in the center almost immediately. It's Jack Frost, her wrists bound in a glittering braid of flaxen rope.

I'm quickly distracted by the elves to either side of her. These elves are locked into their Krampus forms, different from Missy's, but with similar features. They each have horns and those dark, sunken eyes. One has slightly bluer toned skin, the other a dark mauve. They're dressed in tight black clothing, with thick leather straps wrapped around their arms and legs that hold a variety of feathered darts. I'm guessing that's how they secured Jack, with darts dipped in some kind of poison or paralytic.

Jack does look unsteady on her feet at the moment, swaying from side to side as we cross the dark room.

She grins like a demented doll when she sees us coming, leaning forward enough to make the TWAT team seize her upper arms and pull her back. "Hello, Missy," she drawls. "It's been too long. Bad time? You look like you've had a rough night."

My upper lip curls in disgust, and I snap back before I can stop myself. "And you look like a treacherous, desperate has-been, but I'm thinking that's nothing new."

"Ooo, the human has some bite." She says it with a humorous air, but I can sense the anger behind her words, the sharp edge of her pride. "If you're so brave, come a little closer and feel *my* teeth."

Missy steps forward, pushing me behind her. "You won't lay a finger on her."

Jack chuckles softly. She likes the way Missy is reacting to her. "That's the fun part. I don't *need* to use my hands."

I gasp as a wave of ice-cold air blasts me in the face, staggering backward as my eyes sting and the chill nips at my nose. Missy's hand slips out of mine. Another gasp echoes across the room, and the blast of freezing cold suddenly dissipates. I blink a few times, trying to see through a wave of wind-triggered tears, and I balk when I see Missy with one Krampus hand wrapped around Jack's throat. Jack's smile deepens, but then Missy's claws dig into the sides of her neck, and it disappears.

Missy manages to keep her Krampus contained to that one hand as she snarls, "You hurt her in any way, and it'll be the last thing you ever do."

"Don't tell me you're getting *attached* to that thing, Missy." When she doesn't respond, Jack gives her a caustic look, her perfect lower lip pouting. "My stars... I almost pity you, just for that."

"I don't care what you think of me. Not anymore." Missy releases Jack's neck before slowly backing away. She pauses a few feet back, her voice quieting to a dull murmur. "In fact, I think I'd prefer it if you never thought of me again."

Then, she turns on her heel and walks right up to me.

My eye catches on Jack as she begins to fight the TWAT, but they simply tighten their grip on her and force her to her knees. "Missy, don't you even think about it," she growls.

"It's too late, Jack. You made me do this after all the trouble you caused tonight. You're a threat to our planet." Missy's expression is indecipherable when she reaches me. Her gaze lifts to mine, and she takes my hands in her own as her cool demeanor melts.

She gives me a gentle smile, letting me know that what she feels for me is unchanged.

"You *can't*," Jack shouts behind her as she fights the hands on her to no avail. "My family will find a way to retaliate, mark my words."

"Someone shut her up, please," Missy tosses over her shoulder.

The TWAT elves burst into motion. One of them shifts to stand behind Jack, taking control of both her arms as the other pulls a bundle of fabric out of their pocket and stuffs it into Jack's mouth.

Missy turns my face away from Jack with a single finger, guiding my attention down to her. She caresses my cheek with gentle admiration. Then, she slides her hand across my jaw and into my hair, pulling me into a slow but deliberate kiss. Just a few moments of warmth before she breaks away.

She leans into me, holding me, pressing her lips to my ear. "Close your eyes, precious. And keep them closed until I tell you otherwise."

"Why?" I gasp, breathless.

"Try to trust me. Okay?"

When I nod and let my eyes slide shut, she hums her approval, kissing the skin beneath my ear. Her hand slips into the pocket of her father's jacket. She's searching for something. "Whatever you do," she warns as her hand pulls away, "don't peek."

I try not to. I really do.

But by the time I hear her footsteps pad to the other side of the room, I'm peering through squinted eyes. I can't see much in this lighting, but I see enough. Jack is jerking and writhing in her constraints. Missy holds up a device between them, then leans in to say something only Jack can hear. Jack doesn't seem pleased by it. Then, her features start to empty...like she's no longer fully here. A soft ticking echoes toward me, emanating from that device in Missy's hand, and a foreboding tingle crawls its way up my spine. My stomach churns.

I'm not brave enough to keep watching. I let my eyes snap shut again.

There's a flash of light.

Missy's voice breaks the following silence. "You two have done excellent work tonight. Now, go home to your families."

The shuffle of leather soles against wood fills the room as the elves cross the room toward me. Then, I feel Missy's hands touching my face. "You can open your eyes now, precious."

When I do, I see the two TWAT members skirting around Missy and me to reach the staircase. Jack is nowhere to be found.

"What happened to her?" I dare to ask.

Missy's brow furrows. "Does it matter?"

*Maybe.* Because I have this terrible feeling in the pit of my stomach that what just happened to Jack might happen to me. But maybe that's simply my bruised heart talking. "I don't know," I reply honestly.

She hesitates, lips pursing in thought. But then she says, "I made her forget I ever loved her."

My scalp prickles. "Why?"

"Because she's a threat to my world and to *you*." She traces my lower lip with her thumb, smiling faintly. "And I need to protect you both. I can't help it."

I have no response to that.

I want to press her for more information about that device and where the rest of this night is going, but how can I pry after she said something so...sweet? Instead, I lean forward and kiss her, and she embraces me tightly, kissing me a second and third and fourth time.

I'm dizzy by the time she pulls away.

Missy smiles and takes my hand, tugging me toward the staircase. "Come on. Now that all that unpleasantness is over, I'll show you around town."

# CHAPTER 12

# *Nicole*

As we walk the empty streets, Missy points out all the little closed shops.

The North Pole has the same storefronts you would see in a human town, but with a few unique additions: a shop that specializes in magical ornaments that glow and swirl with ethereal lights, a place that carries supplies for unconventional pets, including sweater vests for rabbits and bedazzled collars for polar bears, and a quaint bar that serves a variety of spiked cocoas. Then, there are some shops that carry the most unusual items, almost *alien* in appearance. I notice Missy doesn't explain those ones. It makes sense, I suppose. Santa sort of *is* an alien.

The streets are barely wide enough for us to walk comfortably side-by-side, which makes all the little buildings feel like they are towering over us. It's a comforting sensation, cozy.

"I'm sorry you can't get the full experience of our town tonight. Everything closes for Christmas, and they won't open again for several days," Missy informs me, her soft hand squeezing mine as we continue down the street. We're headed toward the workshop at the end of this lane—a two-story log building standing a head above the rest of the town.

"That's okay," I murmur. "I wouldn't expect anyone to work on Christmas."

Even though *I* did. Even elves take a break, and it makes me realize just how hard I've been pushing myself this last year, working weekends and holidays. Even when I wasn't working, I was thinking about what I had to do. Here, they shut everything down. They stay home. They have to put the work aside. And clearly, it works for them.

The North Pole is thriving. It's infamous.

Meanwhile, I've been working myself to the bone, and I've never felt more forgettable. I'm getting divorced. My mom and dad have given up on me. My niece only knows me through pictures. And my sister... The closest thing we have to a relationship is the picture she keeps of the two of us on her mantle.

Building the life I desire won't mean anything unless I can share it with someone.

And who do I have?

If the entire world shut down, who would I retreat home to? I hate that an abysmal darkness swirls in my mind instead of a face.

By the time we reach the workshop, I've officially retreated so far into the depths of my own shortcomings that I don't realize Missy is trying to get my attention until her hands cup my face. I blink a few times, coming back to myself.

Missy's elegantly arched silver eyebrows are furrowed. "Are you okay?"

I exhale heavily. "Yeah, I'm just...thinking."

"What about?"

I shrug, unable to find the words. All those feelings are brimming on the tip of my tongue, but they're stuck. They are as thick as molasses. I think I might sooner choke on them than let them out, so instead, I take her hands and fake a smile. "Nothing important. I'm ready to see the workshop. Let's go."

Missy's lips flatten into a displeased line, but she allows me to lead the way up the wooden steps to the front of the workshop. Then, she takes the lead and opens the door to usher me inside.

Pleasant warmth wraps around us as we cross the threshold.

I stop in my tracks when I realize the workshop is a hundred times larger on the inside than it looked on the outside, just like Santa's present bag.

The floor drops down in the belly of the room, and dozens of work tables fill its spherical center. Several spiral staircases are placed around the circumference of the space, leading to the second level of the building, which seems to be a catwalk filled with bookcases, small copper machines, and twinkling lights.

Missy closes the front door and ambles to a small table at the end of the entryway, where two black mugs spew steam into the air. She picks them up and turns to me, extending one. "Here. Drink this. It'll help you relax."

I take the mug, eyeing it suspiciously. "Is this going to put me to sleep?"

Because I don't want to fall sleep yet. I don't want to leave this place—or her. I don't want to miss out on even one second together.

She smiles. "No. Dozy cocoa is more like..." She pauses to think. "Like a multivitamin, as your kind would say, brewed with herbs found exclusively in the North Pole. It nourishes. You'll feel better, warmer, maybe a little tipsy, considering this is your first time. It won't knock you out, though."

I lift the mug to my lips, blowing softly on the hot surface before taking a sip.

The cocoa coats my tongue, thick and creamy, with the faintest hint of peppermint and some other earthy herb I can't identify. I moan. The chocolate is dark and rich and sweet without overwhelming the softer notes of flavor that blossom beneath it. A tart, fruity aftertaste tingles on the tip of my tongue.

"This is, without a doubt, the best cocoa I've ever had."

Glancing up, I see that Missy is watching me, a smirk tugging at her rosy lips. She steps forward and hooks her arm in mine. "We've had an eternity to get it right. Our elven perfectionism serves us well."

She leads me past the small table into the rest of the room.

My gaze is drawn to the ceiling, where hundreds of items float mid-air. Wrapping paper, tags, and shiny bows spin slowly, as if patiently waiting for a toy to be tossed toward them. Between the wrapping supplies, a sea of silver glitter twinkles above us too. That silver fills the empty space, wrapped around the railings and threaded into the carpet. The workstations are decked out in colorful Christmas decor, with tinsel and pine wreaths and ornaments in varied hues.

"We have a contest every year for the best-dressed table," Missy informs me, having seen where my eyes drifted. She nods at one of the tables sparkling with pink and purple, a giant golden cup sitting atop it for everyone to see. "The winner gets to decorate our workshop for the next season."

"That's fun; though if the winning table is any indication, you'll be washing pink glitter out of every crease of your body by this time next year," I laugh. "Are the elves competitive?"

Missy smiles and leans into me. "*Competitive* is an understatement. It can get fairly hostile around here, but I also get lots of bribes near judging time, so it's hard to complain."

"Santa, taking bribes?" I click my tongue. "The dark side of the North Pole is frightening."

She sighs. "I only take the delicious ones, and I promise, they have absolutely *no* influence in my final decision...unless there's hazelnut. I'm easily manipulated with a hazelnut cookie."

"Oh, really? I'm taking note of that," I murmur.

Missy peers at me with a coy grin. "Just so long as you don't spread that information around. The North Pole couldn't handle me on a hazelnut high. Disaster will ensue. Reindeer will flee. Bakers will riot. All the hazelnuts in our realm will be used up, and then we'll be snowballed."

I pull my arm out of hers and wrap it around her back instead, tugging her close.

"My lips are sealed, so you can save those hazelnut highs for me." I kiss her cheek, and she hums at the affection.

We ascend the short steps on the far side of the room, and Missy goes rigid in my arms.

Her eyes take on a strange glassiness, and I follow her gaze to a dark wooden door. Colorful filigree is painted along the edges in green and red and gold.

Missy swallows hard and drops her attention to her mug, from which she then takes a long sip. What has her so worked up?

"What is it?" I ask. "What's behind that door?"

"That's my papa's private workshop." Her eyes drift back to the door as if by instinct, as if with longing.

"Can I see it?"

Missy's head whips back toward me, and her wide eyes search my face. I smile, shrugging to let her know that it's okay to say no. I didn't ask for myself. I just have this feeling in my gut that *she's* the one who wants to see it, that she has been telling herself no for a long while. Sometimes, it's easier to do something scary when it's for someone else, especially if it's a thing we secretly desire too.

Missy composes herself and nods slowly, setting her mug down on a nearby workstation before threading her fingers through mine. "I'd love to show you."

# CHAPTER 13
## *Missy*

My father's office looks exactly the way I remember it, and yet, it's different. I don't feel excitement as I look upon the magical items filling the shelves, the framed blueprints covering the walls, the desk in the center that is still cluttered with the pieces of his last project. I just feel empty.

Because the thing I most looked forward to seeing in this room is gone, and it's never coming back. It's just a room.

I turn my attention to Nicole as she takes in my father's life for the first time. She inches toward the nearest bookshelf, reaching out to trace the curve of a glass orb—an outdated version of the time sphere that spins within the sleigh's engine. The magic has been waning from this one for quite some time. Only a faint thread of blue light continues to swirl within the orb's boundaries. Her fingertips graze past the orb to a row of books. They're nothing special, just old volumes filled with North Pole history, but she stares at them with a certain twinkle in her eyes.

I feel the smallest burst of pride warm my chest.

Nicole continues her investigation of the room, and I follow close behind, letting her enthusiasm infect me. I let her poison kill my numbness, and as the pain sinks in, I'm grateful for it. Her attention and admiration bring the memories attached to this room back to life. She touches the old shelves and walls, and it stirs pinpricks of light in my soul.

My chest aches with longing for the things I will never experience again. Sitting at my father's side as he tinkers with his inventions. Sharing milk and cookies with my brother as I help him study the protocols of his Claus birthright. He always struggled to dedicate time and energy to it, even as children, but Father could never pry those old books out of my hand.

This life was my dream, but after all the family sacrificed to get me here, the Claus birthright has lost its luster. I didn't realize how much resentment I carried as a result until now.

I still love the North Pole. I love the magic. I love my new purpose.

I just wish I could have had it all. I would have rather had my family—my father and my siblings still here, with me. I would have rather been unhappy, uncertain of my future, than alone.

"This picture is beautiful. Is that you and your dad?"

Tugged by Nicole's voice, I turn to find her bent over my father's desk, pointing at a picture frame near one corner.

I join her behind the desk.

In the picture, my father is sitting at this very same desk, in his large oval chair, and I'm sitting on the edge of his desk beside him, a tool in my hand and a toothy smile on my face. His kind eyes burn into me. He's wearing his trusty overalls, and his beard is braided with my hair ribbons.

I smile. "Yes, that's my father and me. This was just before my little sister was born. My father dragged me along on all his duties for that entire orbit—my mother was sick, and I was too young to be left alone. She picked up some sort of virus from the human world that wouldn't leave her alone, being mostly human herself. She died in childbirth the very next season. Auntie Mags stepped in to take care of me and my sister after that, but she could hardly keep me away from the workshop. Something about those months at my father's side just...*stuck* with me."

Nicole steps closer, caressing my back. "I think it's very telling that the only picture in this room is one of you and him," she says gently. "It's like he always knew you would take up his mantle, even if he never voiced it."

The truth of her words slams into me. I blink rapidly as tears fill my eyes, but they brim over before I can stop them. "I never thought about it like that," I choke out.

I lean in to look at the photo a little closer.

My father is looking at me, and this is the first time I've ever seen the pride in his eyes, in his smile. He was so happy to have me at his side. Could it be true? Did he suspect I was the true heir of the Claus birthright?

The thought brings with it an indescribable wave of peace.

Nicole is still watching me, so I straighten and return her stare. She inches close and swipes a tear from my cheek with her thumb. "I wish I could take a picture of you right now."

I laugh. "A picture?"

She averts her eyes, glancing again at the picture on the desk before letting her gaze wander to the rest of the room. "I used to take pictures all the time, of anything, everything," she explains slowly. "I had this old camera my father gave me, and I carried it around with me for most of my childhood. I must have taken millions of pictures of my family. Happy. Together. When my father left, I took my camera out to the backyard and pummeled it with a baseball bat. Then, I took the hard drive with all the photos I'd taken of our family and burned it in a fire pit. Some of them my sister had copies of, but most were lost. I wish I could return to that day. I would have saved the pictures. I would have saved my camera."

I nod, turning around to sit on the edge of the desk. "You never thought about getting a new one?"

Nicole shrugs. "It was more than a camera to me. It was what the camera meant, who it came from. I was so angry with my dad that I tried to destroy every connection between us. I was too young to realize people are complicated. I set aside my passion because it was, in part, a piece of *him*. I couldn't separate the two. Sometimes, I still think I'll never be able to."

"That must have been hard."

A sad smile twists her lips. "I did it to myself."

"Still," I insisted. "I know what it's like to feel loss when doing the things I love the most. It makes living true to yourself harder...but more meaningful too, I think."

She huffed a quiet laugh, shaking her head. "You know, when my marriage ended, I thought my life was over. But then I realized I'd stopped living a long time ago. I'd been frozen. There were years of my life I wasted because I had forgotten myself. The night he left, I cried and screamed and tore our whole apartment to shreds. I ripped up the fake life I'd built. Then, I mourned on the kitchen floor until all the wine in our pantry was gone and I ran out of glassware to shatter. When I finally looked up, I saw that the sun was rising. Time was still ticking by. And in that moment, I realized that what I was going through wasn't just an ending. It was a beginning, and I could either choose to embrace it, or I could keep sitting on my kitchen floor surrounded by broken glass and my unhappiness. I wish I could say my unhappiness faded when I stood, but it didn't. But despite my anger and fear and despair, I did it. I moved on with time. I think that's all that matters, in the end. Living, even when you don't want to, even when you aren't sure what living means to you anymore."

There it is. That glimmer of believer, finally rising to the surface.

I reach forward and brush a dark curl out of her face, and her eyes meet mine. "You should do what you love again, Nicole, even if it makes you sad sometimes. Buy a new camera. Search for the beauty in everything. Capture it."

Her breath catches. "My passion is leading me somewhere else at this particular moment."

I raise my eyebrows, somewhat stunned by the blatant lust in her words, and then she's kissing me. Her lips are plush and eager, and they taste like chocolate.

*Addicting.*

I want to sink my teeth into her skin and devour her piece by piece. I have to force my Krampus to stay contained. My dark form wants out. It wants to possess her, own her. It wants to keep her here forever. My own little human to love, spoil, and protect.

I can't give my Krampus control, though. It'll scare her.

Humans aren't accustomed to our intense elven instincts. We're more animal than human when it comes to mating.

Nicole wraps her arms around my back, drawing me into her, and I let my body relax into hers. Her skin is warm and soft, and I suddenly want to know what her arousal tastes like. I want to know what it *feels* like mixing with mine. When her tongue prods its way into my mouth, I wrap my lips around it and suck, combing my fingers into her messy bun and tugging.

Her breathless moan rattles through me, raw enough to take my breath away.

She presses me more firmly against the desk, and I know I need to redirect these activities to the house before we wind up naked on top of my father's forgotten work.

This office isn't mine. Not yet.

I turn my body without breaking our kiss and begin backpedaling my way to the door.

Nicole follows without a fight, her arms still banded around my abdomen, but she pulls away slightly as we stumble over the carpet and collide with the wall. "Where are you going?" she whispers, her voice throaty with desire.

I offer her a grin as my hand blindly reaches for the doorknob. "I have plans for you that require a more *comfortable* environment." And a few special toys, of course.

# CHAPTER 14

# *Nicole*

Missy leads me out of her father's office and into a hallway masked by a rolling jukebox and red curtains. The corridor continues for several feet before we pass through a second set of curtains and enter a large, dark room. The heady scent of pine and cinnamon tickles the edge of my senses.

The only thing I can see with clarity is the snowy tundra glowing through the windows directly across from us, tall evergreens and stray reindeer dotting the landscape.

Then, a switch is flicked to my left, and electric lamps flutter to life around us, illuminating the space. There's a kitchen to the right and the living room straight ahead. I bite down on a shiver as we walk in. It's chilly in here. The wall of windows is likely to blame. But there's also a large stone fireplace in the living room that Missy immediately heads toward after letting go of my hand, allowing me to roam around on my own.

Garlands of pine needles and red berries hang on every available surface—on the tables and counters and the rugged stone mantle, and even wrapped tightly around the wooden staircase railings at the far end of the kitchen. Other than that and a decorated tree standing in the living room, the house seems rather ordinary.

The living room is painted a light sage green, and the kitchen boasts accents of red and gold. The Christmas cheer here in here is soft, understated. Not at all what I expected. But maybe I shouldn't have expected anything in particular—I don't think they celebrate Christmas here, not like Earth does. This is simply what their world looks like. I notice the hints of black throughout the room as well. The black and white pictures hanging on the walls. The ebony carpet in the living room. The macabre knick-knacks sitting on the shelves beside me.

I choke on a gasp when I see the corpse of a fairy, seemingly embalmed within a shadow box.

Missy pauses on her way to the fireplace, reaching behind the Christmas tree to turn on its lights by twisting one of the bulbs. Then, she turns to see what I'm staring at. "Ah, yes. Don't worry, that little sprite met a natural end before I stumbled upon it. It seemed like a pity to waste her beauty in death. Now, she's something of a good luck charm to me. I've had her since I was a very young elfling." Then, she kneels beside the fireplace and begins stacking pieces of wood in the hearth, as if the sight of a real-life fairy—or sprite, like she said—isn't a shock in and of itself.

"You could have used her luck in the sleigh tonight, I think," I mutter.

Missy smiles at me over her shoulder. "That's true. I'll keep that in mind for next year."

I ruminate on which of the many questions floating around my head to ask first. I settle on, "How long has it been since you were an elfling?" I'm just now realizing that she could be hundreds or thousands of years old. If Santa is an eternal figure, how long do elves live?

She seems to hear my unspoken curiosity and smirks.

"I've been alive for quite some time, Nicole. Time works differently here. When our stars are aligned with Earth, I age at the same rate as a human, but time practically stands still once the stars burst and we begin our orbit. Anyone who resides on this planet experiences a longer lifetime because of that."

"So that would make you..."

"In human years, I believe I'd be coming up on my 10,957th birthday."

My jaw drops, and Missy laughs.

"But by elf standards, I am still young," she clarifies, her blue eyes twinkling with firelight as the flame in the hearth grows larger.

My head spins as I absorb that. "My god. How are you—"

She holds up a hand covered in soot. "Before you jump to conclusions, you should know that the length of our orbits feels much shorter than the year you experience on Earth. Like I said, the passage of time is different here. I imagine I *am* quite a bit older than you, but not by nearly eleven thousand years."

I try to make sense of her words, but they're a bit of a mind fuck.

She laughs again then stands and brushes the soot off her hands, leaving behind black streaks on her red trousers. "Don't think about it too hard, precious. It is difficult to make sense of such magic, and even the best wizards of our realm are perplexed by the design of our alignment. It simply *is*. You are not the first world we have served. There have been many before you, and there will be others afterward."

It takes me a moment to decipher her statement, momentarily distracted by the fact that she called me precious again. It makes me *feel* precious.

Then, I start to understand.

After our world dies, she means. She outlives *worlds*.

"Right," I choke out. "So, how *did* this whole Santa thing begin? One day, an elf just happened to realize that your world aligns with others? Then they decided to give everyone on the planet presents just for fun? Is this a hobby to your kind?"

My words sound harsher than I intend them to be, but it's a valid question. What are we to her? What am I?

Missy purses her lips. A certain light creeps into her eyes, a certain *knowingness*. "The greatest magic—the root of my kin's power—is compassion. That is how we create, how we live. If *you* were to see someone suffering, younglings especially, wouldn't you try to make it better in any way you could? Some think gifts are trivial, but they're not. A meaningful gift can convince someone that they matter, that someone sees what they long for and who they are, what is important to them. For just one day, they feel known. And that feeling lingers long after the holiday is gone. Humans who believe in Christmas are really just believing in themselves. That they can hold on for another day, another season, another year. That they can experience joy again, despite the hardships they endure. It is a privilege to be a part of that. It is an honor to inspire those who want to give up. However our duty began, that dream was at the heart of it."

I rake in a deep breath, letting the warmth of her beliefs fill me up like helium. "That's...beautiful. If it's true."

"It is."

For a few long moments, we just stand there, staring at each other. Discomfort and uncertainty weaves between us.

I shift on my feet as Missy looks me up and down. Her expression is passively pleasant but difficult to read. She didn't lead me upstairs, where I'm assuming her bedroom is, so does that mean she doesn't want to take things further? Is she keeping me at a distance on purpose?

The connection I feel with her is like nothing I've ever felt before, and I think that goes beyond Christmas. Something inside me recognizes her, feels at home with her. Tomorrow, I'll be back on Earth, in my mother's house, *alone.* Right now, tonight, though, I'm in the North Pole, surrounded by magic beyond my wildest dreams. I'm standing in front of a beautiful elven woman who seems to see through to my innermost being with ease. I want to see how deep this feeling can go, but only if she wants that too.

"What now?" I whisper.

She grimaces, glancing down at her clothes. "I should take a shower. I'm fairly certain I still have puke in my hair."

"Oh," I mumble. "Okay."

I duck my head to hide the embarrassment warming my cheeks and perch on the edge of the couch. Why did she even bring me here? To show me the most incredible place in the universe and then leave me alone in her living room while she gets all wet and sudsy somewhere else?

This is a unique form of torture. But I am on the naughty list, so maybe I deserve it.

"Nicole?"

My head snaps up at the dulcet cadence of her voice.

Missy leans forward over the threshold of the bathroom, her hands braced on either side of the doorframe. A wicked smile twists her lips to one side. Her body is stretched taut and her red shirt is riding up, revealing a sliver of her tattooed abdomen. I admire the slope of her hips and the valleys on either side of her soft belly. She's so fucking sexy.

My stomach tightens, and I have to clear my throat in order to respond. "Yes?"

She peers at me through heavy lids, her stark-white eyelashes fluttering. "Join me?"

Join her? In the shower? My heart rockets into outer space, and my stomach does a triple backflip into a pool of lava. *Fuck yes.*

Missy sees the answer in my eyes and slips away, beckoning me after her with a smirk.

As I step into the washroom, a thousand or more twinkling lights flicker on.

Multicolored string lights have been hung on the ceiling. They droop along the top of each wall and crisscross chaotically overhead. There are lamps built into the wall above the mirror, but every lightbulb has been pulled from those sockets in favor of the string lights. The twinkling red, green, and blue lights cast the small room in a dim, soothing glow.

I close the door behind us. The reindeer roaming outside don't get to watch this. I want Missy all to myself right now.

Missy leans into the shower and turns the water on, taking her time adjusting the temperature. When she finally turns around and her eyes meet mine, there's a hot lump in my throat. I haven't done anything like this in a long time.

I'm about to have a one-night stand...with *Santa.*

Missy chuckles softly, effectively breaking the tension. "Don't be nervous," she whispers, grasping the hem of her shirt and peeling it over her head in one smooth motion. She drops it on the counter and then unbuckles the belt on her trousers. As she kicks off her boots and wiggles out of her pants, I drink in the silver lingerie set hugging her curves. It matches her tinsel hair, glistening softly under the string lights in the bathroom. She looks like a star.

I suddenly find it hard to swallow. Her body is delectable, her pale skin luminous and adorned with ink. As she steps forward, her eyes drop pointedly to my clothes, and my mouth dries up.

*My turn.*

I peel her father's coat off my shoulders, folding it gently on the counter before facing her. I'm nervous. I can't help it. It's been years since my last first time with someone. I've gotten older since then. I have wrinkles and cellulite and stretch marks now. And *she* is flawless.

Raking in a deep breath, I slowly slide my leggings down my thighs, watching her reaction with my heart pounding in my throat. A welcome wave of excitement surges through me as her eyes fill with hunger. She inches forward. I didn't wear a bra tonight, but somehow, her heated stare gives me the courage to pull my tank top off without another moment of hesitation. My nipples are hard, dark and puckering.

Missy smiles, unabashedly appreciating my chest.

Then, with a breathless noise that makes my core clench, she closes the distance between us, launching up on the balls of her feet to wrap her arms around my neck. She kisses me so forcefully, I stagger back.

My hands clutch her waist then glide up her back as she pushes me against the wall.

I can't help but shudder when her warm body presses into mine. Our curves meld together, every hill finding a valley, every swell discovering a shore. We crash into each other like atoms. I'm shattering, getting lost in her gravity and reassembling myself within the stellar nebula that is her embrace. She's my Milky Way.

One Big Bang, and I exist again.

There is nothing I want more than to stay here in this moment with her, preferably forever. I need to touch more of her. I just might die if I don't do it right now, and I don't know if I could ever forgive myself for dying before knowing how she tastes.

Even if I have to lose her tomorrow.

I shift my hands to Missy's hips and press a thigh between her legs. As her fingers dig into my hair, I force her hips down, guiding her cunt over my thigh. She moans at the friction, and the sound sets fire to my skin.

Catching on to my desires, she devours me. Her tongue plunges into my mouth, sweeping and flicking as she grinds against me harder. Her fingers fist in my hair. My fingertips dig into the flesh of her ass. Her lips shift to my jaw, then my neck. She kisses my skin with the perfect suction, her teeth grazing with delicious precision along my carotid, and I just know I'm going to wake up with hickeys in the morning.

That excites me more than it probably should.

I want to be marked by her.

Missy nips her way across my collarbone before dipping her tongue into the hollow at the base of my throat. My back arches. My head kicks back against the wall, and my eyes close as I drown in the sensation of her mouth against my skin. Her hands cup my breasts, kneading them roughly as her kisses trail down my sternum. Then, she pushes my tits together and buries her face between them. She hums, and the sound reverberates through my ribcage. Her tongue blazes across my sensitive nipples, circling and flicking, teasing me ruthlessly until her teeth finally sink into one.

I whimper, threading my fingers into her silky hair.

She continues ravaging my breasts with her mouth, but my attention is drawn lower when her fingertips dance across my belly, brushing the waistband of my cotton panties.

It figures I would finally get laid while wearing my tightie-whities.

Missy doesn't seem to mind, though. I cease to care myself as she slips her hand under the waistband and explores the throbbing ache between my legs. Her nails sift through my curls, applying just enough pressure along my seam to drive me crazy—my body bucks in desperation. I tilt my hips toward her, and her fingertips find my clit.

She rubs the swollen bundle of nerves skillfully, making my mouth salivate and my skin break out in goosebumps.

I take her face in my hands and drag her lips back to mine.

Her palm wraps around my throat and pushes me back, her nails turning to claws on either side of my neck. Pain furrows the grayish-blue skin between her eyebrows. The usual rosy tone of her complexion and the moon side of her nature battle across her features, her Krampus tickling just beneath the surface.

She's so beautiful like that, hovering between dark and light.

Missy gazes up at me with a slack jaw and sharpened canines. When I lean forward, she tightens her grip on my neck to stop me, shaking her head as the furrow in her forehead deepens.

"What is it?" I whisper, my worry bleeding through the words.

She closes her eyes and shakes her head again. "I just need a moment to compose myself. I'm too close to losing control."

"Lose it, then."

Missy's eyes flash open, her head bobbing back in surprise. When she sees I mean it, she swallows audibly. "You don't understand how intense the shift can be when sex is involved, precious. I don't want to scare you."

I smiled, tracing lines up and down her spine. "I'm not scared, Missy. I want all of you."

A wave of relief ripples over her. She softens her grip on my throat while her other hand shifts to my hair. Carefully hooking a claw into my hairband, she cuts the elastic tie, and my curls fall around my shoulders. She draws my dark hair forward to frame my face, smiling softly.

Missy's gaze makes my spine tingle, so doting and tender and warm—a sharp contrast to her shifting grey skin and the horns budding on the crown of her head.

Dropping her claws to my panties, she rips through the white fabric, and it falls away. She looks down the length of my body, seemingly captivated by the dark curls between my thighs. The horns on her head lengthen and curl into dangerous points.

Then, she speaks, and the words are laced with dominance. "Shower."

I barely recognize her voice, raw and deepened with desire, but I obey it without a second thought. Turning toward the shower, I'm met with my reflection. I'm also gifted with the view of Missy bending over to glide her panties down her legs. I fight against every yearning fiber of my body—the ones begging me to turn around and fall to my knees behind her—and enter the small, tiled shower. The warm shower spray engulfs my side, and steam pebbles across my skin.

I revel in the cascading water for a moment, watching through the frosted glass as Missy's blurry silhouette reaches back and frees her breasts from the silver bralette.

Then, she turns and enters the shower behind me, and I twist to greet her with a smile.

My breath steals out of my chest when I see her. She's an absolute vision, probably the most stunning woman I've ever seen.

*No*—she is. Nothing and no one compares to the creature standing in front of me.

Her Krampus horns are still visible, but the rest of her body has shifted back to a warmer complexion, her puckered nipples a dusky pink against her otherwise pale skin. Tattoos stretch across her stomach and up over her ribs. These tattoos are different from the rest, and I find it fitting that they seem to reflect her more monstrous form. Winged insects and flowers weave through a stylized animal skull, a forked tongue emerging from its mouth. It's no animal skull I'm familiar with, so it must be a creature that lives here in the North Pole.

Or perhaps it's a Krampus skull, I suddenly realize.

I want to kiss every single inch of her belly, just to know what the ink feels like beneath my tongue. The smirk Missy gives me when she notices my distraction is enough to push me over the edge. I yank her into my arms, kissing her soundly before she has a chance to react, before she has a chance to take control. I pin her up against the wall of the shower, and she gasps in surprise, goosebumps spreading across her skin from the cold surface. I take that opportunity to slide my tongue between her lips.

I want more. I *need* more.

I drop into a crouch, my face level with her bare, slender-lipped pussy. Pushing her knees apart, I lean forward and slide my tongue through the peak of her slit, my eyes fluttering as her arousal fills my senses. She's slick and hot. I can feel her pulse throbbing through her center. My tongue rolls over her clit as I lift her knee over my shoulder, spreading her wide. I savor the guttural groan she makes as I lick her opening. Then, I thrust my tongue into her to hear it again.

Digging my fingers into her hips to hold her in place, I attempt to devour her very soul.

Missy fingers thread through my hair, her claws gently scratching my scalp as she presses my mouth more firmly against her. She's already close. I can sense it in the trembling of her thighs, the sharpening pitch of her moans. Then, her pleasure bursts, and she comes in my mouth.

I drink down every bit of her and then pull away to meet her stare.

She has surrendered wholly to the Krampus. Her skin is dark gray, and her horns are larger than I've seen them. The bones of her skeleton are closer to the surface somehow, beveled, visible through her skin.

Without taking her eyes off me, she reaches over and turns off the shower.

Missy doesn't pause to grab a towel for either of us. She simply pulls me along behind her, both of us soaking wet, out of the washroom and into the living room. The moment we step over the threshold, she flicks her wrist, and several of her macabre knick-knacks come to life, flying off the shelves towards the couch. Stuffed bats and broken angel statues and creepy old dolls leap onto the cushions, grabbing the blankets and throw pillows from the furniture. They drag the soft layers to the floor and arrange them in front of the fireplace.

By the time we reach the hearth, the knick-knacks have finished their task and start returning to their shelves.

My eyes lock with Missy's, her eyes burning like blue fire. She spins us around so I have my back to the soft bedding, and before I can catch my breath, she pushes me. I fall into the thick nest of blankets, and she follows me down, kneeling between my legs. Shoving my knees apart, she looks at the triangle of curls between my thighs and growls deep in her chest. As her lips part, I see her canines have elongated. She doesn't look like a Christmas elf right now. She looks like the sort of creature who would live on the edge of a forbidden forest, beckoning you into her deadly embrace with wicked smiles and promises of unthinkable power.

The elves who live in the North Pole are *real*, and the

shadows that live within each human lives within them too. They're a little bit scary, but they're magnificent.

Missy's sharp claws graze along my slit, and I gasp in surprise, my body stiffening as she carefully caresses my slick lips. Then, her hand shifts. She continues with her knuckles, applying glorious pressure against my clit. My hips twitch as I groan, and she grips my hip firmly, forcing me to remain still as she kneads my aching nerves, circling and rubbing while I pant at the ceiling.

"Oh my God," I whine. "Please, Missy. *Please.*"

She stops touching me, and I could have cried at the throb between my legs as Missy leans over me, capturing my full attention. A cool tingle spreads across my body when I see the look in her eyes. There's anger here. Or...frustration, maybe.

Missy bares her teeth and says, "You want to know what really squishes my sugar plums, Nicole?"

I tentatively nod, a prickle of fear dancing across my nape of my neck.

"No one ever thanks Santa. Not really. It's always *please* this and *please* that. It's only ever begging and wanting and endless demands." Her head tilts to one side, an animalistic quality to the motion. "Do you think that's *nice?*"

My heart starts hammering against my ribs. I swallow the acrid dread sticking in the back of my throat and shake my head.

Missy smiles. "I'm a giver, precious, but you damn well better realize that I'm going to be thanked for it. Think you can handle that?"

With some effort, I manage to nod again.

"Use your words."

I clear my throat and lick my dry lips, fear and arousal thickening the blood in my veins. "Yes."

Her smile grows, her jaw slackening as a thick, black

tongue slithers out of her mouth. It curls in mid-air, long and flexible and forked at the very tip. She leans forward and licks up the column of my neck, her tongue swirling over the shell of my ear.

My body shudders.

"I want to give you pleasure, but I need you to do something for me in return." She slips a fist between my thighs again, stroking my clit.

"Anything," I choke out.

"I expect you to thank me for each one of your orgasms. *Loudly.*"

"Yes, yes," I exhale shakily, "whatever you want."

Missy chuckles softly then peels away from me, her hand and the heat of her breath disappearing from my skin.

My eyes flash open, and I rise on my forearms, trying to follow her wherever she's going, but she spreads a hand over the center of my chest. She pushes me back down into the blankets. "Don't move. I have to go get something, and I want you to stay here."

My brow furrows. I don't want her to leave.

She sees the desperation in my eyes and shakes her head, smirking as she grabs one of my hands and drags it to the ache between my legs. "Keep playing with yourself while I'm gone. Don't stop. If you stop, I'll be very angry with you. Understand?"

"I understand."

"And don't come. That belongs to me." Her gaze sears into me, serious and starving.

"Okay," I whisper.

Missy glances pointedly at my hand, and I start circling my clit, the sensation pulling a long moan from my lungs. Satisfied with my obedience, Missy stands. I'm only vaguely aware of her walking away, my attention torn in several directions, but then her voice cuts through the static. "And Nicole? One more thing."

I pry my eyes open and see her standing on the bottom step of the staircase. "Yes?"

She gives me an uncertain smile, and I think she might be *nervous*. "Think of me."

*God help me.*

"No problem," I say, grinning cheekily as she takes off up the stairs. It would be impossible to *not* think of her. Of that wicked Krampus tongue filling my pussy. Of her silken hair in my hands and her body draped over mine.

I lose myself to the fantasies.

It's a struggle keeping myself from the edge of ecstasy, but I manage it, if only barely. My whole body is trembling by the time I hear her return, my fingers soaked with my own arousal.

Missy kneels beside me, setting a short, red velvet box on the floor next to our nest of blankets. She unlatches the lock and flips the top open. A long column of silicone sits inside. It looks like a...candy cane? Red and white silicone spirals down its length.

As she lifts the item out of the box, I realize what it is.

A candy-cane colored silicone sex toy. One side is shaped like a typical vibrator, but the other side curves slightly and has a short, bulbous tip. The way it's shaped... I think *both of us* are supposed to use it. At the *same time*.

Nervous butterflies fill my stomach, my pulse fluttering wildly as she crawls back between my legs with the toy in hand.

She pushes my hand away and grazes a knuckle across my lips, smiling when she finds me soaked. "You are so wet, Nicole." The way she says my name makes me want to cry. Cry and come and cry. "Needy and wet. Exactly what I wanted."

Missy turns the dildo in her hands and then lines up the short, bulbous side with my entrance.

She starts kneading my clit as she circles the bulge into my channel, pressing in only an inch before withdrawing. As she does that again, her fingers move more firmly against where I throb.

My back arches off the floor, and Missy lightens her touch.

Her long tongue trails across my chest, twirling around and flicking my nipples. She hums in appreciation. "Say please again, precious. Tell me what you want."

"*Please*. Please make me come."

"And you're going to thank me, yes?"

"Yes, Miss Claus." I pull her down for a kiss, and her hands continue their impeccable work until I'm crying my release into her mouth. My pussy gushes, covering the toy and Missy's hand.

Missy grasps my chin with her free hand and leans back, forcing me to look at her.

"Thank you," I sob. "Thank you, baby."

As I continue coming down, Missy removes the dildo, and I bite back a wince. Everything is extra sensitive right now. It has been a while. "That's it," she purrs.

She lifts the toy in front of her to admire my glistening cum.

I don't think I've ever been called perfect before, not like this. Her praise is going straight to my head—I'm light-headed and warm and tingly all over.

I watch in some kind of pleasure-addled fugue state as Missy leans back and spreads her legs right there in front of me, holding herself up with one hand as she brings the dildo to her pussy with the other. Her jaw slackens, her Krampus tongue rolling over her chin as she pushes the bulbous end—the same end that was just inside me—into her channel. She moans as she maneuvers the toy deeper, bending it to her liking.

When the dildo is placed, Missy falls forward, catching herself on one palm as she hovers over top of me. Her eyes are crescent blue moons. The rest of her body is sharp and dark and rough...but those eyes. There's a deep, heart-wrenching affection in them. She's drunk on my pleasure.

Seeing her this turned on by it makes me borderline frantic.

I grab her by the face and kiss her deeply, desperate to feel as much of her as humanly possible. My knees hook over her hips as she shifts between my legs. Then, there's a hard bulge sliding up and down my slit, gathering moisture before pushing in. We both groan at the intense pressure. Her hips twitch and thrust, as desperate as I am.

I'd be okay if she decides to ruin me. I want her to.

Missy breaks our kiss and leans up, rolling her hips to push deeper inside of me. Her expression is hard as granite, *focused*. It's the hottest thing I've ever seen. Her abdomen flexes with each thrust. Her tattooed skin shines with a thin layer of sweat. Her silver hair cascades over her shoulders and down her chest, her pink nipples barely peeking through.

My core trembles under the weight of my arousal.

"You want to see why this is my favorite toy?" she purrs. The sweetness of her voice is almost enough to do me in, but I hold out for her.

"Why?" I gasp.

She reaches between us, her fingers massaging my tight entrance. With a surge of power, the dildo starts vibrating. The rest of the world falls away. Our hips jerk and writhe together in a maddened, urgent race for release until I can't hold on any longer. My body detonates.

"*Thank you*," I rasp between the waves of pleasure.

The first peak is barely past when the friction of Missy's pussy rubbing against mine is enough to push me over the edge again. I'm coming hard again, whispering my thanks and begging for mercy. I can't handle much more. I'm going to combust in a fiery explosion of blood and stardust...or at least, that's how I imagine death might look like in the North Pole.

Missy stiffens with a low moan, melting on top of me, and the toy falls still between us.

Santa kisses the soft skin beneath my ear and whispers, "The naughty list is wrong about you, precious. You're such a good, good girl."

AFTER EXHAUSTING OURSELVES, we settle in under the blankets to rest, Missy's body nestled against my side and her head on my chest.

I stare out the windows at the purple-tinted tundra.

"Does the sun ever rise here?" I wonder aloud. It should be the middle of the day right now, but the sky is pitch black.

"The sun will rise when the stars burst," Missy replies, her voice small and lined with exhaustion, a stark contrast to the demanding vixen who rode me for the second time just minutes ago. "Christmas Day is a time for darkness, for rest."

I run my fingers through her hair, appreciating how soft and silky the strands are. "I'm sad I won't get to see it in the daylight."

"Me too. At least you got to see it. Very few watchers ever do."

Missy's eyes glaze over as her mind wanders from our little cocoon in front of the fireplace. The turn in our conversation bothers her, and I can guess why. I've been piecing together the truth all night, and I think I finally have it figured out. She's going to make me forget her somehow before sending me home. Jack Frost implied it. Auntie Mags too.

I can't say I blame her for that decision. I'm only a watcher to Missy, even if she's quickly becoming much more than Santa to me.

The truth isn't enough to stop my falling for her. I'll take whatever she offers me, even if my feelings have to be erased by morning. It was enough just to experience this. It was enough to live and love as deeply as I have tonight. And at least if my memories are taken, I won't have to miss her. Just the thought of missing her for the rest of my life makes my eyes sting.

I duck my head to hide the tears and swirl my fingertips over Missy's lower belly. Leaning in, I start trailing kisses down the column of her neck, letting the salt on her skin tingle across my tongue.

My affection drags her back to me. Our future is pushed away into the horizon.

Missy laughs, the twinkle of her voice flaming the fire in my belly. "Aren't you tired, precious?"

"I still have one last thing I want to do before this day is over."

Missy's brows furrow in confusion, so I smile and turn so my body is hovering over hers, my face dropping to nuzzle her bare chest.

Parting my lips, I let my tongue slide over a plane of black ink on the outside of her breast, and then I pucker my lips and blow cool air on the damp skin. Her tattoo and the skin all around it erupts in goosebumps, and I lean forward to kiss it. "One," I announce with a devious grin.

I move on to the tattoo next to the first and repeat my unhurried process. "Two."

Missy face dissolves in pleasure as I travel lower, and she lets herself melt into the pillows as I kiss my way down her torso. Her little mewling sounds grow louder as I caress the insides of her thighs, as I kiss a constellation of stars on her hip.

"*Eleven.* Now, I need you to remember that number for me, Miss Claus."

Her breathing is labored as she smirks down at me. "And why is that?"

I blow on the slick lips between her thighs, and her eyes flutter. "Because I'm going to lose myself in you now," I inform her. "And I don't know when I'm coming back."

# CHAPTER 15

# Nicole

When I finally force my heavy eyes open, I realize I fell asleep. In the next breath, I remember where I am. In the North Pole. In the circle of Santa's arms.

I'm still Cinderella, and the clock is still ticking down to midnight.

I jerk upright, groggily taking in my surroundings. The fireplace is gently crackling, but it's burning lower now. When I see the pitch darkness lingering outside, I exhale in relief, and the panic coiled tight in my belly loosens—it's not too late to go home. I have no idea how long we've been sleeping, though. A long while, I'd be willing to bet.

My gaze drifts to the elf slumbering next to me.

Her Krampus is gone. Every inch of her body is warm and soft, her complexion pinkish gold, her hair shimmering silver in the firelight. The relaxed pucker of her lips does things to me. I want to lean in and count every last eyelash resting on her cheeks. I want to pull the blankets away from her sweet body and wake her up with my mouth, but I force myself to stay right where I am.

Missy begins to stir, and I quickly slip out from beneath the blankets before she reaches for me. I've stayed long enough as it is.

What was I thinking?

Sex was one thing, but catching real feelings for a total stranger? For Santa Claus? Sleep has given me some much-needed distance and *perspective*. What was the point of this if I have to forget it? Bitterness is setting in, and I can't shake it. I suddenly wish I hadn't come here. I wish I had thrown Missy out of my mother's house and allowed her to save Christmas by herself.

My chest tightens under the weight of those thoughts.

I don't mean them. Not really. I'm just scared.

This brief fairytale we shared is ending, and I am fucking terrified. I haven't lost Missy yet, but I already miss her. And I have the strangest intuition that this will be permanent. That even if she does take my memories, this feeling in the pit of my stomach will always remain. She changed me. How am I ever supposed to be happy again? What if I miss her like this for the rest of my life and I don't even realize it? Nothing will ever compare, no one else will ever measure up, and my heart will know. How could it not?

As I push myself to my feet, Missy's eyes open.

She frowns as I gather my clothes from the bathroom and start dressing. "Is everything alright? What's wrong?"

I throw her a fake smile as I wiggle into my leggings. "I'm just getting ready to leave."

"Yes, I can see that." She sits up, her frown deepening as I return to the living room with my slippers in hand. I perch on the edge of the couch and slip the fuzzy pink monstrosities onto my feet. Then, I shrug my jacket on and zip it up, avoiding eye contact.

If I look at her, those blue eyes will pull me in again, and I can't let that happen.

But the longer I don't look at her, the more obvious my upset becomes. The silence screams everything I can't voice. After a few agonizing moments, Missy stands, and I squeeze my eyes shut as she approaches. She's still naked and too beautiful to be real. Her hand gently cups my chin and tilts my face toward her.

"Stay."

My eyes snap open, and I meet Missy's stare. That one word sends tingles racing throughout my abdomen.

"Stay?" I mutter. "What do you mean, *stay*?"

Her thumb caresses the line of my jaw. A nervous smile trembles on her lips. "I know we've only just met. I know this is sudden, but think about it. You could stay here for a whole human year, with me. You could do something that makes you happy. You're good with toys. You're good with deliveries. Help me organize the elves and prepare for next Christmas, and I promise to arrange for your other job to be waiting for you when we return to Earth, if you want to go back."

It takes my brain a long moment to comprehend what she's saying, and by the time she stops talking, I've officially started panicking.

I brush her hand from my face and scramble off the couch, putting some space between us. I pace between the living room and kitchen instead, shaking my head to clear it. "You can't offer me something like this, Missy."

She steps forward but thankfully keeps her distance. "Why not?"

"It's not a good idea," I say forcefully, glancing her way. I immediately regret it, because she's not hiding even an ounce of her feelings. Her brow is bunched and her eyes are slanted in sadness. I just have to rip off the Band-Aid. Indulging this fantasy won't help either of us. I can't stay here. I *can't*. Inhaling deeply, I brace myself for what I need to say. "This whole night has been one bad idea after another, and this might be the worst idea of all."

Missy blinks a few times, her lips flattening in a hard line. "How could you say that?"

"I'm not good enough for you," I shout.

"What are you talking about?" she demands, her own voice rising. "You were there tonight. You felt it. We're good together."

I laugh bitterly. "I'm on the naughty list, *Santa*. Not only am I human, which means I already don't belong here, in the jolliest place in the universe, but I'm a *bad* human. I'm a loser. I work on Christmas Eve, for fuck's sake."

"So do I," she argues.

I speak over her, needing her to hear me, needing her to *understand*. "I smash people's prized possessions when they piss me off," I remind her. "I make sad women cry in fraternity bathrooms. I'm no good, and you know that. You're Santa. You don't belong with someone like me."

Missy's eyes glaze over as her hands fall limp at her sides.

After a long minute, she scoffs and turns on her heel, disappearing into the bathroom before re-emerging with her father's coat. She pulls it on and draws the sides closed, shielding herself. I hurt her, and I hate that I hurt her. I hate that our fairytale is turning into a grim tragedy right before my eyes.

I sigh. "Missy..."

"What I *know*," she cuts me off with razor-sharp authority, "is that getting on the naughty list has nothing to do with morality, Nicole. You aren't on the naughty list because you're a bad person. You're there because you're too damn scared to open up to anyone, so you just push them away instead. But what's worse is that you push *yourself* away. You are a stranger to your own heart. How can anyone give you a gift that means something when you don't know what you want? You don't let anyone see who you are, yourself included."

My lips flap as I search for a response. "You're wrong. I–"

Missy closes in on me, her eyes watery and sparkling with anger. "What do you want, then? Do you want me, or do you not? Forget that I'm Santa. Forget everything that you believe is standing between us and just tell me the truth. From your heart."

Maybe I *should* know the answer. Maybe she's right, and I don't know myself at all. Maybe I became someone else entirely in the pursuit of a relationship that was never meant to be.

But that also means I have no business starting something new.

"I don't think I know what the truth is," I tell her.

She nods, sensing my honesty. Her voice softens as she asks, "What was last night to you? Was it real? When you wake up in your mother's house, will you believe me to be a dream?"

A small glimmer of hope ignites, warming my chest. Those questions make me think she might actually let me remember all this, and if that's true...

I shake my head, reaching forward to brush a thumb over her rosy cheek. "My dreams are never this sweet."

She closes her eyes, briefly savoring my touch.

"We'll find out soon enough," Missy whispers. She pulls a small, star-like instrument out of her father's coat and raises it between us. I don't remember that being in the coat when I was wearing it earlier. The center of the star starts glowing, illuminating the tears in Missy's eyes. "Be a good girl, Nicole. Let the love in, and when you're finally full again, give it to someone else."

"What is that thing? What are you doing?" I demand

tremulously. She can't be making me forget. She *can't*. Not after giving me hope that she wouldn't.

I reach for the instrument.

Missy's tears brim over as she whispers, "Goodbye, Nicole." And a burst of blinding white-blue light fills my eyes.

# CHAPTER 16

# Missy

"You didn't wipe her memory?" Auntie Mags screeches as she follows me out of the house quarters. The stars are just about to burst, and she stopped by to make sure Nicole had been sent home in time. Her relief quickly evaporated when I told her I let Nicole remember what happened last night. "What were you thinking, Missy? That human knows far too much."

I sigh heavily, rolling my eyes as I brush aside the curtain at the end of the transitional hallway and enter the workshop. "And what exactly do you think she's going to *do* with that knowledge?"

"I don't know," Mags growls, stomping over the threshold. "She could tell her world's scientists about our alignment or, heaven forbid, write a *book* about us. It took centuries to convince these humans we were a myth after the last watcher returned home with their mind intact. Deliveries were perilous for a decade. Hunters organized, humans became insufferable just to prove a point. Your father was careful about this for a reason."

Spinning on my heel, I nail Mags with a scorching glare. "Mama was a watcher."

Auntie Mags deflates a bit, her features softening at the mention of my mother. They were very close for many orbits, practically sisters by the time she died. "Yes, she was. But Missy...she stayed on our planet at your father's behest. This is hardly the same thing."

My gaze drops to the floor. "I asked Nicole..."

"You asked her what? To *stay*?"

I clench my hands, restraining my Krampus as I remember how painful her rejection was. "Yes. I asked her to stay, and she didn't."

Mags doesn't respond right away, and when I look up, her expression is thoughtful.

"Just say it," I tell her.

She tilts her head back and forth, seeming to consider the idea of Nicole living here. "I did sense a certain thread of magic in her, albeit deeply buried."

I swallow hard. I'd felt that too. Thinking about it now makes my blood run cold, though. I broke every Claus protocol with her, *for her*. I gave her my all without question, without hesitation. I fell headfirst. There has to be a reason for that. Something in me recognized something in her.

But all I can feel at the moment is my regret.

"Forget it," I mutter. "I don't believe Nicole will speak a word about us to anyone, and if she does, she will frame it as a colorful dream, the way all humans speak of world crossings."

I turn to leave, but Auntie stops me by placing a hand on my shoulder, her arm barring my path.

"Just tell me this," she says quietly. "When you're with her, does it feel eternal?"

The eternal is all I know. It's familiar. But it is another thing entirely to sense the eternal in a human...and I did with

Nicole. It happens. It happened to my father. It has happened many times to our ancestors, through different galaxies and with dozens of unique, intelligent species. The Void has a way of forging these unusual unions over and over again.

I nod. "I believe it could be, but that means nothing if she cannot believe in herself."

"That is true." Mags squeezes my shoulder. "Give it some time, my dear. See how much she grows during our next orbit. Maybe the stars just need to realign."

Smiling weakly, I shrug out from under her touch, silently dismissing her as I approach the door to my father's office—*my* office, I remind myself. It's time for me to properly claim it.

Before I can change my mind, I slip into the office, facing the door as I close it. I rest my forehead there for a moment, breathing in the woodsy cinnamon scent clinging to the walls. Papa loved burning cinnamon candles.

When I turn around, I have a plan.

With brisk determination, I cross the room and scoop up the outdated time orb from the shelf. I carry it with me to the desk, hesitating for only a moment before I take a seat in the oversized velvet armchair, accepting my fate as a lump lodges itself in my throat. After rifling through the drawers for what else I need, I lay out my tools and get to work.

The tears fall.

I let them flow. I let myself feel everything. I let myself feel extraordinarily sorry for myself, knowing this might be my last chance to do so. The North Pole needs me. The elves need me. The worlds that will never fully appreciate what we do for them...they need me too. All I have is the rest of this night, and then, the orbit begins again. My life's work begins. And this year, I will let myself be grateful for it.

I will still carry this sadness, of course, but I will learn to embrace happiness again too.

Through bleary eyes, I manage to solder a sturdy clasp onto the orb and braid a loop of twine to thread through it. Then, I lift the sphere to examine how smoothly it swings from side to side.

*Perfect.*

My magic has waned after the activities of the last couple days, and because of our proximity to Earth, it won't start regenerating until the stars burst. But I have just enough left to do what I must. I'm not going to count on Nicole changing her mind by next year. I'll only wind up crushed again if I do. So, this is my farewell, and it has to be a good one.

I press the orb to my chest and exhale slowly, allowing my magic to wrap around it.

The metal and glass fractures, turning from solid to liquid to gas in a matter of milliseconds. The colored gas seeps through my fingers and rises, swirling above my head like a blue-tinted rain cloud, waiting. I glance at the window, knowing I need to give the gas a route out, but I hesitate. There's something missing. The gift feels...*incomplete.*

Warm, orange light dances on the horizon. I'm nearly out of time.

I let my gaze drift to the desk, to the photo sitting on the edge. I may have shown Nicole an entire world and beyond, but she changed the way I looked at my own world, the way I looked at my life. Perhaps my father did know. Perhaps he suspected where my passions lived and where my brother's didn't.

Reaching across the desk, I pick up the picture frame and press it to my chest, closing my eyes as I summon the last dredges of my magic.

Heat and cool pleasure tingle under my skin like liquid peppermint. Blue smoke fizzles out of my pores and lifts to join the cloud waiting on the ceiling. I blink up at it, smiling with damp cheeks. This will have to be enough.

Setting down the picture, I push myself away from the desk and cross the room to the window. I turn the old brass knobs and tug the window pane up. A cold breeze sweeps in, and the atmosphere in the room shifts, kicking up a tornado within the cloud of magic. The spiraling cloud funnels through the window and into the night sky.

I blink, and the magic is gone. I'm empty. Barren. Cavernous.

I'm ready now, for whatever comes next.

The stars overhead blur, seeming to vibrate as the light on the horizon grows brighter. They don't really explode. *We* are the ones vibrating. Our entire planet shakes as it slips out of alignment, and the atmosphere charges with energy until I'm breathing static.

Behind me, the electronics in the room flicker on and off. My father had collected musical novelties throughout his existence. A handful of holographic music players from several planets past light up, and an old wooden radio from Earth starts buzzing.

The sky flares with a brilliant red light.

I squeeze my eyes shut, waiting for our planet to settle into place in a cosmos far, far from the Milky Way. When the light outside dulls, I let my eyes flutter open again. I take in the blue sunrise, the violet streaks of light painting the morning sky.

With a sigh, I tug the window pane down. And that's when I hear the music.

*I'll be home for Christmas....*

*You can count on me...*

I slowly turn, my limbs filling with lead. I know that song. Papa used to gather me and my siblings in his office for breakfast cocoa after his deliveries, and we would listen to the human radio until this song played or the stars burst, whichever came first. The song continues, tinny and undulating with static, but I'm gobsmacked because...it shouldn't be playing at all.

Earth's radios shouldn't work here.

A shiver crawls up my back, and cool air prickles my arm. It feels like something or *someone* is standing next to me, but when I look, nothing is there. The room is empty, save for the memories.

I smile, and fresh tears flood my eyes as I whisper, "I love you too, Papa. Merry Christmas."

# CHAPTER 17

# Nicole

I remember it all.

I remember my Christmas Eve flying through the sky on a magical sleigh. The frat house with all the stolen toys that came alive. My run-in with Jack Frost. That never-ending night of passion in the North Pole with Krampus claws wrapped around my neck.

I remember Missy, and my heart aches.

For whatever reason, she let me keep my memories, and I can't decide whether it was intended as a gift or punishment. Either way, I think I deserve it.

I spent three days and nights staring at the sky, waiting for a miracle I knew in my heart would never appear. Missy is hidden on a planet galaxies away, and she's not coming back. Not until next year.

My mom returned home this morning and dragged me out of my bed, and now, I'm helping her take apart the Christmas tree. Full. Fucking. Circle. I do my best to master my emotions. If I burst into tears here, she'll never leave me alone, so I force myself to feel everything beneath the surface.

Seeing these perfect glass ornaments hanging on the tree makes me sick to my stomach. It's like that night never happened. This is why I stayed in the bedroom for as long as possible. I didn't want to be reminded of what Missy did for me, how she took the broken shards of my heart and reassembled them, reminded me of what it felt like to fight for myself, and then vanished into the stars like some sort of phantom.

And I won't lie. I considered the possibility that it was all a fantastical dream for all of one minute before her words returned to me.

*Will you believe me to be a dream?*

*My dreams are never this sweet.*

She is real, even if the only place she exists on this planet is in my head. I won't let go of her. I won't make her smaller for my own comfort.

As I lift a sparkly red star off the tree, I announce, "I'm quitting my job."

My mom pauses where she's bent over on the other side of the tree, her head slowly leaning around the dusty white limbs to stare at me. "What did you say? I couldn't have heard you right."

I push the star ornament into its plastic packaging and turn back to the tree to find its twin, trying to act as nonchalant as I can manage with my mother glaring at me like I just sprouted Krampus horns. "I'm taking this next year off. I might do some consulting on the side so I don't go totally broke, but I really want to..." I search for the right words then chuckle to myself when I realize those words are: "do nothing"

There's a long moment of silence, and then my mom exhales.

"Oh honey," she begins, her voice full of pride. "I think that's a wonderful idea. Time away from work is precisely what you need. Are you going back home to work things out with Matt?"

Not even the mention of my self-centered ex can sour my mood. For the first time in a long time, I have clarity.

I shake my head. "I called Dad."

Mom tenses, her shoulders bunching around her ears as she sits back on the floor. I've shocked her. The deep furrow on her forehead tells me she's at least a little bit insulted too. I can't remember the last time anyone mentioned Dad in front of her.

In her silence, I explain, "He said I could stay with him and his wife. They have an old shop I can convert into an apartment, and it's close to Grace. I called her too."

She blinks, distracted from her anger by that last omission. "You *did*?"

I nod. "We have plans for next Saturday. I'm going over there for dinner with her family." I smile as I remember hearing Abigail in the background of our phone call, screaming at the top of her lungs, filling the stunned silence after Grace recognized my voice.

*I told you so, Mommy! I told you she wanted to see us!*

An ornament dangles forgotten from Mom's fingers as she absorbs this information. It's not every day something leaves her speechless, but then her features unexpectedly soften, like a thousand tons are being lifted from her shoulders. She's *relieved*.

Without warning, her chin starts trembling. "Oh...Nicky," she warbles, practically slapping herself in the face with the ornament as she covers her face with her hands and cries.

I quickly round the tree, dropping to my knees at her side. "Mom, I'm sorry. I didn't mean to upset you." My hand hovers above her shoulder, wanting to comfort her but not entirely certain why she's melting down. She could be furious with me.

She could think I've betrayed her by talking to Dad behind her back.

She shakes her head, peering at me over her fingertips. "No, Nicky. I'm just so *glad.*"

"You...aren't angry?"

"You called your sister!" she exclaims. "How could I possibly be angry with you ever again?"

I laugh, knowing she'll eat those words within the day but grateful for the unexpected support. Leaning forward, I give her a hug. It's awkward but nice. It has been years since I last hugged her, which is easy to do, considering my mother doesn't particularly enjoy affection.

Mom returns my hug, blubbering against my shoulder as she pats my back, that forgotten ornament bouncing against my ribs. "I love you, honey. I'm so proud of you."

I wonder if this is why she *really* wanted me to go back to Matt, because I'd already shut her and the rest of my family out of my life, and he was all I had left. All I *let* myself have. Maybe she just didn't want me to be alone. Despite her faults, my mom has her good moments too, and I'm thankful this is one of them.

Clearing my throat, I manage to choke out an, "I love you too."

Then, I pull away, returning to my work on the opposite side of the tree so she can't see the tears in my eyes. My anxious heart has its limits.

After a few more minutes of working together in silence, I hear my mom gasp. She kneels on the floor and ducks her head under the tree. "Did you get me a present?"

"Huh?"

I definitely didn't, but I circle the tree to look at what she pulls out. It's a shiny green package with white ribbons.

"You left a present underneath the tree? Why didn't you say anything?" The joy in her smile is enough to make me lie.

"Oh, I—uh, I wanted it to be a surprise."

Mom flips the tag over, scanning it, and laughs. "From a Missy Santa Claus. That's clever. You really tuned into the Christmas spirit while I was away, didn't you? You even wrapped a second present for yourself."

She leans down and pulls out a second box from beneath the tree, this one wrapped in metallic pink paper and a bright red bow. My name is written in large, thick lettering on the red tag.

I take it from her, my heart thundering.

The other side of the tag reads, *We both know I can't give you what you really want for Christmas, but I hope this helps bridge the gap between what was and what can still be.*

I amble my way to the couch, my legs numb from the shock of having the evidence of her existence right here in my hands, the myth who stole my heart. The sound of my mom ripping through wrapping paper is muted, as if she's rooms away. For a moment, I'm completely alone.

Then, I carefully pull on the ribbons securing my package, intending to keep every scrap of her as intact as I can. They're precious.

When I finally manage to remove the many folds of wrapping paper, I wiggle a white box out and place it on my lap. My box is larger than my mother's. I look up and catch a glimpse of the ornament she's squealing over—and I recognize it as one of the items that had been sitting in Santa's private workshop. The magic that swirled inside of it is gone. Now, it's just a pretty glass ball. The magic will probably only come back once the North Pole is aligned with us again. As my mom leaps up to put her gift on the tree, I return my attention to my own.

I open the box and fall utterly still. I forget how to even breathe.

It's a camera, exactly like the one my father gave me, with a creamy white case, a detachable lens, and an ink-stained, extendable flash on top. I don't know how Missy did it, but it looks just right.

A trembling smile tugs at my lips as I lift the camera out of the box.

I could cry at how perfect it feels in my hands, how the plastic is already worn down, like satin against my fingertips. Twisting the knob on top, the camera turns on. The screen lights up a dark blue, shifting to a live visual of the camera lens, but then an alert pops up on the screen.

*MEMORY FULL!*

Brow furrowing, I navigate to the playback, and a picture appears. It's the one that was sitting on Grace's mantle, of me and her as children, our arms wrapped around each other. I thought the original was gone forever, but here it is. In my hands. In the corner of the screen, the camera states that this is the last photo out of thousands. Unable to stop myself, I start to look through the others, and goosebumps prickle up the back of my neck.

Every picture I lost, all the ones I destroyed in anger... They're here. Pictures of my mom and dad back when they still loved each other, pictures of my sister and me when we still trusted each other. Memories I thought were lost.

Missy gave them back to me.

A feeling expands in my chest, warming me from the inside out. She loves me. I know it as surely as I know the sun will rise every morning. The memories of the time we spent together were a gift, just as these are a present to the girl I used to be. The girl who destroyed everything she touched just to know she could still feel *something*.

Hurting was easier than healing, but I'm stronger now.

Next year, when our planets align on Christmas Eve, I'm

going to be make sure I'm healed enough to give her everything she wants, everything she *deserves*. I just hope I won't be too late.

January 1st, 2023

Dear Missy Claus,

New Year's Eve was actually really fun this year. I spent the evening at my sister's house, and we watched the fireworks from her backyard. The kids tried hard to stay up, but they ended up falling asleep on the trampoline. I think our game of "crack the egg" really tuckered them out. I played with some of the extended capture settings on my camera when the city's light show started, and I caught some awesome shots of the sky! It reminded me of the falling stars surrounding The North Pole.

I miss you already.

Yours,
Nicole

February 14th, 2023

My dear Miss Claus,

Has the pink glitter invaded all your orifices yet? I don't know if the North Pole celebrates Valentine's Day, but there's only one Valentine I want this year, so I'm hoping you'll be mine. Consider the hazelnut cookie included in this letter to be an official bribe. Miss you.

Still yours,
Nicole

May 1st, 2023

Dearest Santa,

Spring is here! I have about a thousand photos of my Dad's tulip garden. It's so beautiful here this time of year. Do you have seasons in The North Pole? Flowers? I wish you would write me back. I have so many things I'd like to ask you.

~~Are you happy?~~

~~Do you miss me too?~~

I've also finally gotten the word out about my little photography hobby, and I'm taking family photos for some of my sister's friends. I can't help but think of you as I do it, though. I see these couples, so in love and committed and growing these beautiful families... and I miss you. I want to believe they could be us someday, somehow.

Truly Yours,
Nicole

October 12th, 2023

Missy...

I really, really wish I could see you today.

Forever yours,
Nicole

December 3rd, 2023

Dear Miss Santa Claus,
I know you're getting a lot of letters this time of year, but I don't think I could stop writing even if I wanted. This is the only way I can hold on to you, even if it is one-sided.

I wanted you to know I figured out what I want this year.

I just want to see you.
Just one more time, on Christmas Eve. Don't be late.

Yours,
Nicole

# CHAPTER 18

# Nicole

## ONE YEAR LATER - CHRISTMAS EVE

"*Shhh*," I hiss over my shoulder as Abigail and I tiptoe downstairs, my camera hanging around my neck. "If you wake your mother, she's going to scold us both."

Abigail's cherub smile lights up the dark. "I can be quiet. *You shhhh.*"

I laugh under my breath and nod, taking the small hand she extends to me. First, we sneak into the kitchen and swipe a few cookies and cold milk. Then, we carry them into the living room. We set the plate and cup on the coffee table before settling in on the couch, facing the fireplace. The lights from the Christmas tree softly illuminate the entire room.

When Abigail is halfway through the cookie in her hand, she turns to me, chocolate staining her fingers and face. "What if Santa doesn't come? What if she forgot where we live?"

I smile. "Santa never forgets about good kids, and you're a good kid, Abigail."

She nods, soothed by that simple explanation, and finishes her cookie.

I'd told her the truth, and I had confidence that Missy

would show up for Abigail, even if she wanted nothing to do with me. I'd sent hundreds of letters to Santa over the last year, and while I had no way of knowing if they were being delivered or read, I had enough faith to hold out hope, even if I hadn't heard a single word in return.

Abigail insisted on staying up with me tonight, and I couldn't bear telling her no, even if I have to carry her to bed in a few minutes when she inevitably falls asleep. I cherish every moment I have with her.

Being around her reminds me of how easy it is to find joy in the small things.

"How does Santa's sleigh fly?" she asks after swallowing her final bite of cookie, licking her fingers before wiping them clean on her plaid nightclothes. I cringe at the streaks of brown left behind on her shirt. Grace is going to throttle me for letting her stain her Christmas pajamas.

"Well..." I lean back into the cushions and sigh, recalling the events of last year for the millionth time. "The sleigh is engineered with magically infused parts, but it's like a car. The reindeer help steer the sleigh through the sky, but the actual flying power is maintained by machinery. Everything needs to be properly tuned, or it can be as dangerous as driving a car with faulty parts—you can crash. But you don't have to worry about that, because Santa is trained to fix the sleigh if anything should go wrong. In fact, that happened last year. An elf called Jack Frost tried to tamper with the sleigh, but Santa crawled underneath it mid-air and fixed it."

"Wow." Abigail yawns, her eyes starting to droop. "I hope Jack Frost stays away from the sleigh this year."

I scoff at the ceiling. "Yeah, me too."

I hope Jack Frost stays away from Missy period. It's been a year, though, and who knows what might have happened in that time. Maybe they made up. Maybe they're back together.

That would explain why none of my letters have been returned.

I shake my head, putting those thoughts away.

"In fact," I murmur, pushing myself off the couch and circling the tree, searching for the ornament my mom brought. She wanted to look at it on Christmas, she said. It was a surprisingly sentimental gesture on her part, but that's family. They always surprise you, for better or worse. I find the ornament Missy gave to Mom last year and smile when I see the threads of blue magic twirling within the glass. I carry it back to the couch and hand it to Abigail. Her eyes turn into saucers as she takes in the magical glow. "You see that glow? That means Santa is on her way." Although, Mom didn't seem to see it today when she was admiring it.

Maybe only true believers can see the magic.

Abigail clutches the glass orb to her chest, relaxing into the crook of the couch cushions. Within a handful of minutes, she drifts off to sleep, just like I expected.

"You sneaks."

The whispered words slither in from the stairway, and I twist to find Grace gliding down the final steps into the living room.

I lift my hands in surrender. "Hey, I was simply doing my job as the cool aunt. Letting her stay up past bedtime is my right, and if you have an issue with that, take it up with Auntie Julie. I think there's a Ouija board up in the attic."

Grace rolls her eyes but perches on the armrest of the couch with a smile. I know she doesn't really care about us sneaking down here. "I think it's sweet of you to do this whole Santa thing with Abigail. You made this Christmas really special for her. It's sad to think that pretty soon, she'll be too old to believe in it anymore." She frowns down at her daughter nestled into the corner of the couch.

Her dark brown, curly hair is wild right now—she went to bed without drying it first. We have the same hair, but her eyes are blue like Mom's. She's wearing a matching set of those red plaid pajamas, the wooly material clinging to her lush curves. She has gotten even prettier since we were teenagers, but she looks more at peace now. We've both done a lot of healing this year.

I sit up, cradling my camera against my stomach. "You're never too old to believe in Santa."

Her delicate eyebrows raise. "Is that right? Do you?"

"Don't you?" I ask with a half-smile. "At least a little bit?"

Grace smirks and then looks between me and Abigail as a genuine smile grows out of her amusement. "This year has been incredible, Nicole, having you around like this. Abigail and Corey love you to pieces—we all do. I really missed you."

My heart twinges with the reminder of all the time we lost. "I missed you too."

"Do you have to leave us again so soon?" She grimaces. "I feel like I only just got you back."

I lick my lips, searching for the right response. "It won't be forever," I say slowly. "And I don't even know if the job is going to work out yet, so let's not talk about it."

"You've barely said a word about this year-long trip as it is. I have no idea where you'll even be going, or who exactly you're going with."

"I told you about Missy."

She gives me a withering stare. "You told me about a woman who doesn't seem to exist."

"She exists," I say, a bit more forcefully than I intended.

It's her turn to lift her hands in surrender. She's unaffected by my sharp tone, smiling because she's my little sister, and sometimes, she enjoys ticking me off. "Then maybe you should invite her to Christmas tomorrow."

"Maybe I will," I mutter.

"Good." With that, she stands and turns around to lift her slumbering daughter off the couch. "Night, Nicole. Love you."

"Love you," I whisper to her departing form.

Then, silences falls, and it's filled with all my lingering anxiety and worry, all the fears I cannot voice. What happens if I see Missy again and things have changed between us? What if she fell out of love with me? We've been apart for so long... It's possible.

*Let the love in, and when you're finally full again, give it to someone else.*

I'm ready now, but she's the one I most want to give my love to. So, I have to be brave. I have to have faith in myself. I am worthy of loving and of being loved, and I'll keep hoping it will be with her until she tells me otherwise.

I put away my doubts and wait.

At exactly half-past midnight, I hear something land on the roof. Clopping hooves, tinny bells. I wiggle upright from where I'd sunk back into the couch. I remove the cover from my camera lens and move to a corner of the room where I'm partially hidden but still have a clear view of the tree. Kneeling, I prepare to capture the moment.

Footsteps echo overhead, drawing a line across the roof to the fireplace flue. Then, the atmosphere in the room shifts.

Soot trickles down the flue.

A soft blue glow appears, pouring out of the hearth and gathering like a cloud in front of the mantle. Then, she walks out of it, looking as beautiful as the day I met her.

*Missy.*

Her silver hair glistens as she leaps into action, letting the Santa bag roll off her shoulder and land on the floor in front of the Christmas tree. She hemmed her father's coat—it no longer drags on the ground behind her. Instead of the red shirt she wore last year, she's wearing a dark camisole with lacy black straps and peek-a-boo stripes that show off the tattoos on her abdomen.

As she crouches next to the bag, I snap a picture, the room lighting up from the flash.

She startles, blinking rapidly in my direction as I straighten to my full height in the corner. I step into the light, and her eyes widen as she stands as well. For a few long moments, we just stare at each other. I can't bear to be so far away from her, so I step forward, moving slowly.

"Nicole."

Missy simply says my name, and it's like my entire body comes to life. My limbs begin to tremble, and my heart flutters like a hummingbird's wings.

"Fuck," I exhale. "It's so good to hear your voice."

Her head tilts to one side, almost in agreement, but she doesn't come any closer. She only says, "I got your letters. I think you might have beat out little Timmy Turner for the most Santa letters sent in one year. Pretty impressive, actually."

Her eyes are guarded, but her gaze is intense.

Every day, I wrote to her. And she got the letters. I can't determine whether or not she read them, though, and I can feel my uncertainty scraping against my nerves.

I chuckle nervously, shifting on my feet.

"Yes, well, I had little else to do all year. I don't know if you read any of my letters, but I quit my corporate job. I've been living here in Wyoming, started a small photography business, and I'm feeling...*better*. Thank you for the camera, by the way. I can't tell you how much that meant to me, the pictures especially." I'm rambling now, but I just can't stop. I have to fill the silence with as much about my progress as I can, because then, maybe she'll see I'm good again. Maybe she'll look at me the way she did in the North Pole—like she wants me. "I've uploaded them all to a computer and shared them, so no chance of losing them again. My family was just as excited as I was to have them back."

The ghost of a smile dances across Missy's lips, but then she purses them, as if trying to hold on to her composure. She takes a step away from me, and my heart drops.

She nods at the camera in my hand. "I'm not sure I can let you keep *that* picture."

"Take it with you then," I whisper, taking another step toward her, not caring about anything but sliding back into her orbit. I have faith in what we had. I have faith in myself, and my heart is telling me to leap. "Take *me* with you."

Her perfect rosy lips part, and a shaky breath saws out of her. "Nicole..."

"Please don't," I interrupt, my voice stronger than ever. "Don't say no. Don't leave me here. All I can think about is you, Missy. I get up in the morning, and I wipe dreams of you from my eyes. I take pictures of happy couples and beautiful families every day, but in their place, I imagine *us*—someday, somehow. Don't say no to this, to *us*. Say yes. Give me one more chance to love you."

Missy bursts into motion, crossing the room in a second, and takes my hands in her own. Her composure is crumbling. Gray shadows and her usual rosy complexion battle across her features, and a certain glassiness swims in her eyes.

She speaks, and her voice is a balm to my heart. "I was only going to say that you probably *should* come home with me tonight, seeing as you left your eyeglasses at my house last year."

Then she smiles, and the room around us fades away.

I huff a laugh, pulling her toward me by our conjoined hands. "Classic move, right? I'm so lame."

"No," she disagrees.

The sharpness of that word gives me pause. "No?"

"You are Nicole Strobe," she says, her blue eyes sparkling. "You're 30 years old. You started believing in Santa again exactly one year ago tonight, and from this day forward..." She inches forward slowly, deliberately, until we are chest-to-chest, breathing each other's air. "You're *mine*."

Santa kisses me, and I am lost again to her orbit.

Her tongue slides into my mouth, and I let her take control. I surrender, letting her have every inch she wants of my body and my heart—because it's all already hers.

We somehow manage to stumble our way to the couch, and I don't know how long we lay there kissing and touching and holding one another, but when she finally pulls away, my lips are swollen. I love how she kisses me with the force of a scorching sun, the strength of a beast. It would be a privilege to be kissed by her for the rest of my life.

The rest of my life begins today.

"How do you feel about spending Christmas Day with my family?" I blurt out. "I think they'd like to meet the woman I'm about to disappear with for an entire year."

Missy blinks, equally surprised and delighted by my question.

"I think that sounds perfect, precious." She jumps up and extends a hand to help me off the couch. "I do have a few more continents to deliver presents to first, though. Join me?"

Suck it, Grace. The love of my life is coming to dinner.

I take Santa's hand, grinning so wide that my cheeks ache. "I wouldn't miss it for the world."

# Missy

EPILOGUE

I lounge on a reading chair wrapped up in my long red robe, watching as Nicole bounces and writhes on the toy I set up for her in front of the windows in the living room.

She's gloriously naked, and her arms are tied behind her back with a string of twinkling colored lights.

Her long legs are spread wide for balance, flexing as she carefully slides herself up and down the dildo attached to the floor. Frustration twists her features. She has to move slowly to avoid losing her balance—she's been teetering on the edge of her orgasm for a few minutes now.

A wicked smirk overtakes my face.

I love torturing this woman. Only for our mutual pleasure, of course.

Nicole peels her green eyes open, her stare pleading. "Please, Missy?" Her voice trembles and cracks. She tries not to beg as a general rule, knowing it sometimes rubs me the wrong way, but I've pushed her past her limits today.

I suppose I'll let her get away with it this time.

Rising from my chair, I approach her undulating body. She's not moving with any semblance of rhythm anymore. She put on one hell of a show, stripping naked and grinding against me until she was wet enough to ride the toy, but now, she's tired and needy.

I halt a few inches in front of her and grasp either side of my robe, gently pulling it away from my chest.

Nicole makes a desperate noise as her gaze drifts to my breasts.

"Do you need my help, precious?" I croon.

She nods, her eyes glazing over as I drop the robe entirely and it lands in a silken pool around my feet. "Yes, Miss Claus."

I tilt my head to one side and brace my hands on my hips, considering our options. "It doesn't look like you're helping yourself much at the moment. You'll never come like that."

Her nostrils flare as I step closer.

My pussy is level with her mouth, and I can tell by the way she leans forward that just the taste of me might finally tip her over the edge.

But I don't want our fun to end so soon.

I slide a hand into her dark curls and tug her head back, leaning down to kiss her. My tongue strokes hers, and when she hums, I can *taste* the sound, sweet and warm and wanting. Her back arches, her pretty mauve nipples reaching for me, and I let my other hand drop to squeeze her breast, smiling against her open mouth as she moans. I love her little noises. I love...everything about her, really.

I'm struck with an intense wave of emotion, my love for her mixing with the cutting edge of gratitude. Joy pierces my heart like a lance. Tears gather behind my closed eyes.

Nicole may be bound for my pleasure, but *I* am the one ensnared.

For as long as I live, I am hers. It's decided. And for as long as she lives, I hope she's mine. Whatever time we are given to be together is a gift I won't take for granted. It's too easy to lose the things we love—people, dreams, ourselves. Oftentimes, they are taken away in the blink of an eye, and there's nothing anyone can do to stop it. The resurrection of a heart after unspeakable loss, on the other hand, is the truest, most powerful magic in this universe. Everything means more to a healing heart. Every touch. Every laugh. Every kiss.

It is a privilege to love.

When Nicole whimpers against my mouth, I break our kiss, smirking before I lean over her shoulder and grasp her hips between my palms. I push her down, forcing her to take a few more inches until she's full and gasping. I guide her hips up and down, angling her for more friction against her g-spot, pushing her harder and faster until she's crying my name.

In her desperation, she buries her face between my legs and runs the tip of her tongue along my slit, and I allow it.

I thread my fingers into her hair and let her devour me. Her hips jerk and swivel, unable to stop as her need surpasses the aching muscles. Her tongue swirls over my throbbing clit, and my upper body curls forward at the pleasure, my legs very nearly giving out. I splay a hand on the window to steady myself. Steam spreads out from beneath my palm, whitening the surface of the glass—in fact, this entire windowpane is fogging up.

I lean over Nicole's shoulder again and slide a claw under the string lights to cut them off her wrists. My Krampus has already broken free from its leash.

Nicole likes my Krampus *a lot*.

When her hands snap free, Nicole grabs my hips and tugs me closer, hooking my leg over her shoulder so she has complete access to my center. Her tongue glides easily through my slick, pushing into my entrance and swirling over my clit.

She sucks on the throbbing nerves, making me shriek. I pull on her hair half-heartedly. Her body bounces up and down on the toy, quickening as her eyes roll into the back of her head.

When a deep groan of ecstasy vibrates through my center, I know she's coming.

I grab a fistful of her curls and pull her head back, crouching down to her level as my mouth returns to hers. She slides her tongue between my lips, tasting like my arousal and a hint of the sweet, ambrosial wintergreen berries we ate at dinner. That's a new favorite for Nicole.

Perhaps our food will be enough to convince her to stay for another orbit.

We haven't talked about it—whether she would stay or go. Our current orbit is nearly over, and I have no idea what her plans are for when we realign. She hasn't brought up Christmas yet, and I'm too frightened to ask her outright. I'm trying to be patient. I know how much she misses her family, and I know she'll age at a far slower rate if she continues to live here with me. Eventually, she'll have to stop seeing them. Or worse, she'll keep seeing them for the rest of their lives, and then she'll have to watch them die.

I couldn't ask *anyone* to endure that, but especially not her. Not my love.

Nicole's body is limp in my arms, but I continue kissing her in earnest, savoring every moment of her pliant lips as she returns to herself.

"You are so perfect," I murmur.

She chuckles then grunts softly, wiggling in discomfort at the large toy still buried inside her. Her arms wrap around my neck, and I take the hint, wrapping my arms around her waist to lift her off it. An airy wisp of a moan fills my ear as I kneel, our bodies colliding as I set her down beside me. Her lips trail sweet kisses across my jaw.

But I'm focused on that toy, soaked and glistening with her cum.

I twist in place, burying a hand in Nicole's hair to guide her lips up to mine. Practically panting with desire, I pull her into me, dragging us both upright on our knees. I grasp the toy with my other hand and shift my body to hover over it, the slick tip prodding at my entrance. I lean back to look into her darkened green eyes and purr, "I want you to fuck your cum into me now, precious."

Nicole's returning smile is diabolical.

She wiggles her way closer and drops her hands to my hips, applying enough pressure to force the dildo in an inch. Once she's certain I'm slick enough, she offers no mercy. I feel her fingers starting to bruise my skin as she manipulates my hips, tugging me up and forcing me back down, returning my ruthlessness tenfold. That's one of the things I love the most about her. She takes control when I need to be cared for, when I need a break. This entire orbit, she has been a true partner to me, my helper and lover and friend. My everything.

I quickly find my release with her arms snaked around me and her mouth covering mine. She swallows every last morsel of my pleasure.

We crawl onto the couch and curl up together, a thin blanket draped over our damp bodies, Nicole's fingers combing mindlessly through my hair. I melt into her side, my head resting on her chest and my leg hooked over her hips. This is my favorite place in the entire universe. I've lost count of how many times we've fallen asleep right here, wrapped in each other's arms. I would be happy spending every day of the rest of my existence like this.

If only I was so lucky...

Once our hearts have settled, I sense a change in Nicole. She shifts beneath me, almost uncomfortably. When I glance up at her, I see the cogs turning behind her eyes, the distance in her stare. "What is it?" I ask reluctantly.

She grimaces. "We need to talk, baby."

Here it is. She's breaking up with me. I knew this was coming—there's only a handful of days left until our planet realigns with Earth. I just didn't think it would happen today. This is her choice, though, and I will respect it the same way I respect her.

Bracing myself for the inevitable, I sit up, putting a little more space between us. "Okay," I sigh. "I'm listening."

"I was thinking," she starts, the words tentative and quiet. She's at least as nervous as I am, maybe more. While that might have made me feel better, but I don't want her to hesitate when it comes to her feelings. Even if she's leaving, I want her to feel comfortable around me, no matter what. I grab her hand and hold it tightly, and she manages to get the rest of it out. "Could we spend Christmas Day at my sister's again this year?"

My brow furrows. I wasn't expecting her to plan out another Christmas together, but I'll take every second I can get.

I nod, squeezing her hand a few times in quick succession. "We certainly can. You know how much I enjoyed meeting your family last year. I would love to be included again."

"Good," she murmurs, her eyes straying to our joined hands.

"That's not the only thing you wanted to talk about," I prompt.

When her gaze meets mine again, her eyes shine. "No, it isn't," she admits. "I was wondering if there was a way to get me home early on the morning of Christmas Eve so I can spend the day at my Dad's place? I want to take advantage of the full forty-eight hours we're aligned with Earth, get in as much quality time with them as I can."

"Forty-eight hours?" I echo her words, allowing them to sink in fully. She's talking like...she plans to be *here* for another orbit. "You're not going back home for the year?" I dare to ask.

She blinks rapidly, her face scrunching in confusion.

"Of course not," she declares with fierce conviction, leaning forward to cup my face. Tears sparkle on her lashes. "*Na'pishky.* Wherever *you* are is my home."

I release a heavy breath.

Na'pishky... it means *I love you* in elvish. Nicole has proven to be quite the natural at our language, as if she was born to learn it. Perhaps she was.

All the tension bleeds from my body, and I surge forward to kiss her, a giddy lightness sweeping through my chest as my mouth covers hers. I giggle against her lips, and she smiles. Her arms wrap around me, comforting and soft. She's right. This feels like home.

I simply kiss her for a while, communicating my gratitude and relief and the deep affection I feel for her. Then, I whisper, "Na'pishky, precious. I love you to the Void and beyond."

A soft flush fills her cheeks, and she nuzzles closer, burying her face into my neck.

I let my head fall back against the cushion and close my eyes, resting in stillness as relief cleanses my nerves. She isn't leaving me. She wants to stay. "You know, you just about frightened the stockings right off me," I tell her. "Why were you so nervous bringing that up? I love your family."

"I know you do," she says into the crook of my neck. "I wasn't nervous about *that*. I'm nervous about the question I want to ask next. I'm not sure how you're going to react to it."

I shrug a little to urge her to look at me, and when she lifts her head from my shoulder, I pinch her chin between my thumb and forefinger.

"You can ask me anything," I assure her, staring deeply into her eyes. "*Always*."

She bites her lower lip, and I'm sorely tempted to eat her up myself. But then, with a sigh, she asks, "Would you ever be willing to tell my family who you are? Who you truly are?"

My heart sinks. "I don't know..."

There are Claus protocols to be followed, rules that protect both us and the humans. It's better for them if they believe we are a myth. Panic can destroy a planet as well as any asteroid.

But I would cross every boundary, forsake every law, for my human.

Nicole slips a hand beneath the blanket to touch my hip, leaning into me, seeking my warmth. "I know you usually have to wipe watcher memories, but what if we offered to bring them back here with us? What if they chose to live here? Then, they wouldn't be watchers anymore. We don't have to tell them anytime soon, but they're my family, and maybe, someday down the road, the perfect moment will present itself. I just wanted to know if that has ever been done before. Is it possible?"

Her words are threaded with uncertain hope. She's been thinking about this for a long time. I can't say I fault her for it. Now that she knows the North Pole exists, knows the intimate wonder of our planet and its magic, it's only natural that she would want to share it. She made friends here in the North Pole, more friends than I have, if I'm being perfectly honest. But that's not the same thing as having family around. I know that.

I hesitate, carefully considering her request.

In theory, there's nothing that expressly forbids a human family from moving here. And why couldn't they? We've had a number of species settling here over the many millennia our planet has been orbiting. Our kind has taken many mates.

I inhale deeply, affectionately grazing a thumb over Nicole's cheek. "For you, I will do my best to make it possible."

A brilliant smile lights up her face as she falls forward to embrace me.

I turn my face into her hair, breathing in the intoxicating scent of her shampoo—jasmine and candied strawberry. A sharp wave of fear crashes over me, and I voice my worries before I can stop myself. "You would really rather stay with me, here, forever, instead of living a life in your native galaxy? You'll have to watch everything you've ever known come to an end."

She turns her head, her nose nestling next to mine as she kisses the corner of my mouth.

I feel her head shake gently. "Even forever with you wouldn't be long enough." She leans back suddenly, blinking a couple of times. Then, a chuckle crackles through her, a gentle burble of amusement followed by deep, full-bodied laughter.

"What are you laughing about?" Even bewildered, I can't help but laugh with her.

She shakes her head. "I just realized you're my glass slipper."

"What?"

Nicole wraps her hands around my neck and pulls me in, her eyes softening with desire and...*joy*, I think. "You're my happily ever after, Missy Claus."

My heart skips a beat and then starts pounding hard against the inside of my ribs.

"And it is an honor to love you, Nicole Strobe." I kiss her again, slow and thorough, our tongues tangling. She clings to my arms and allows me to press her down into the couch, her body rolling sensually beneath me as I stroke her thighs and hook her knees up over my hips.

Eventually, I pull away to grin down at her, admiring how the starlight shines through the window and reflects off her dark curls. My own little human. I get to keep her forever.

"Alright, precious. Forget about the nice list and show me just how naughty you can be."


THE END

# Acknowledgments

A huge thank you to my readers. You are all so supportive and so willing to tag along on all my genre hopping, and I wouldn't be able to do this author thing without you.

To my husband, what more can I say that hasn't already been said? You are my biggest fan. I love you.

To my critique partners/beta readers, thank you for your feedback on this sapphic whirlwind! Shannon, Erin, Amanda, Michaela—you guys are amazing.

To my editor, Alexa, thank you for putting up with my last minute changes and many questions.

# About the Author

**Beka Westrup** is a genre-hopping author of fantasy and romance. Little Miss Santa Claws is her seventh publication. She lives in the PNW with her husband and two children, collecting more books than she'll ever be able to read and drinking copious amounts of iced coffee.

Stay in the know with Beka's Newsletter:
https://www.bekawestrup.com/

 facebook.com/bekawestrup

 instagram.com/bekaboowrites

 tiktok.com/@bekabooauthor